A TAKEDOWN

Longarm kicked the lantern and dropped as it went skittering off across the cold tiles without going out like it was supposed to. The infernal machine had been invented with rough handling in mind, and its beam swept in every direction in imitation of a toy lighthouse gone mad whilst Rube Shire blazed away with both sixguns, confounded by the razzle-dazzle effect on his own billowing clouds of cotton-white black-powder smoke, until all of a sudden the beam was stationary, pointing straight up, and Longarm fired once from where he lay on his side on the tiles.

Once was enough when you knew what you were doing . . .

DON'T MISS THESE
ALL-ACTION WESTERN SERIES
FROM THE BERKLEY PUBLISHING GROUP

THE GUNSMITH by J. R. Roberts
Clint Adams was a legend among lawmen, outlaws, and ladies. They called him . . . the Gunsmith.

LONGARM by Tabor Evans
The popular long-running series about Deputy U.S. Marshal Long—his life, his loves, his fight for justice.

SLOCUM by Jake Logan
Today's longest-running action Western. John Slocum rides a deadly trail of hot blood and cold steel.

BUSHWHACKERS by B. J. Lanagan
An action-packed series by the creators of Longarm! The rousing adventures of the most brutal gang of cutthroats ever assembled—Quantrill's Raiders.

DIAMONDBACK by Guy Brewer
Dex Yancey is Diamondback, a Southern gentleman turned con man when his brother cheats him out of the family fortune. Ladies love him. Gamblers hate him. But nobody pulls one over on Dex . . .

WILDGUN by Jack Hanson
The blazing adventures of mountain man Will Barlow—from the creators of Longarm!

TEXAS TRACKER by Tom Calhoun
Meet J.T. Law: the most relentless—and dangerous—manhunter in all Texas. Where sheriffs and posses fail, he's the best man to bring in the most vicious outlaws—for a price.

TABOR EVANS

LONGARM

AND THE UNGRATEFUL GUN

JOVE BOOKS, NEW YORK

THE BERKLEY PUBLISHING GROUP
Published by the Penguin Group
Penguin Group (USA) Inc.
375 Hudson Street, New York, New York 10014, USA
Penguin Group (Canada), 90 Eglinton Avenue East, Suite 700, Toronto, Ontario M4V 3B2, Canada
(a division of Pearson Penguin Canada Inc.)
Penguin Books Ltd., 80 Strand, London WC2R 0RL, England
Penguin Group Ireland, 25 St. Stephen's Green, Dublin 2, Ireland (a division of Penguin Books Ltd.)
Penguin Group (Australia), 250 Camberwell Road, Camberwell, Victoria 3124, Australia
(a division of Pearson Australia Group Pty. Ltd.)
Penguin Books India Pvt. Ltd., 11 Community Centre, Panchsheel Park, New Delhi—110 017, India
Penguin Group (NZ), Cnr. Airborne and Rosedale Roads, Albany, Auckland 1310, New Zealand
(a division of Pearson New Zealand Ltd.)
Penguin Books (South Africa) (Pty.) Ltd., 24 Sturdee Avenue, Rosebank, Johannesburg 2196,
South Africa

Penguin Books Ltd., Registered Offices: 80 Strand, London WC2R 0RL, England

This is a work of fiction. Names, characters, places, and incidents either are the product of the author's imagination or are used fictitiously, and any resemblance to actual persons, living or dead, business establishments, events, or locales is entirely coincidental.

LONGARM AND THE UNGRATEFUL GUN

A Jove Book / published by arrangement with the author

PRINTING HISTORY
Jove edition / February 2006

ISBN: 0-515-14069-4

JOVE®
Jove Books are published by The Berkley Publishing Group,
a division of Penguin Group (USA) Inc.,
375 Hudson Street, New York, New York 10014.
JOVE is a registered trademark of Penguin Group (USA) Inc.
The "J" design is a trademark belonging to Penguin Group (USA) Inc.

PRINTED IN THE UNITED STATES OF AMERICA

10   9   8   7   6   5   4   3   2   1

Chapter 1

The misunderstood Judge Isaac C. Parker was not bloodthirsty. He was efficient. Having federal juristiction over the Indian Territory as well as the Western Federal Disrict of Arkansas he heard the cases of a whole lot of outlaws brought before him by the two hundred deputies of U.S. Marshal James F. Fagan and His Honor only sentenced the more murderous ones to death on his notorious economy-sized gallows.

This ingenious device, operated by the efficient and professional if spooky-looking George Maledon, who prided himself on quick clean deaths, had attracted the attention of eastern newspapers and been unfairly sold as the western answer to old England's seriously macabre "Hanging Judge" Jeffreys. But neither Parker nor Maledon hung 'em by the half dozen to offer the crowd assembled a thrill. A professional hangman and his crew were paid by the hour and it only made common sense to save up condemned criminals until you had enough on hand to make a hanging worth the time and expense.

And so as Deputy U.S. Marshal Custis Long of the Denver District Court arrived at Fort Smith they were fixing to hold such a mass execution just short of a week away.

Slated to drop were Abraham Tenkiller, a Cherokee moonshiner who'd mistaken a neighbor for the law; the white killer, Shorty Baker; Smokey Dave Smith, a wife killer of color; the white partners in rape, Gus Miller and Tex Addams (their victim having been an Indian ward of the federal government), and the famous Frank Hungerford, a hired gun who'd gunned an Indian agent over in The Territory.

It was for Hungerford the Denver District Court had sent Longarm, as he was better known, with a prior federal indictment to save Famous Frank for a less-dramatic hanging in Colorado.

The firm but fair Judge Dickerson down the hall from Longarm's home office ordered them strung up one at a time, albeit it was generally agreed Famous Frank Hungerford was long overdue a hanging.

Judge Parker being off to a Sunday-Go-To-Meeting-On-The-Green with his family when he arrived on a weekend, Longarm got to fuss it out with Marshal Fagan at the Fort Smith lock-up after the head turnkey on duty sent for him.

Fort Smith's answer to Longarm's own boss, Marshal Billy Vail, was a tad younger, in better shape, but just as set in his ways as he read Longarm's writ and declared any judge who'd issue such ass-wipe a total idiot if not in the pay of sinister forces.

Fagan said, "How come they've ordered you to carry Hungerford all the the way back to Colorado, spend time and money trying him for an earlier killing and then hang him, when old George was just getting set to hang the son of a bitch *here*, before you'll ever get him back to Colorado?"

Longarm shrugged and said, "You may have just answered that when you described his Colorado killings as *earlier*, Marshal. I agree the mills of Miss Blind Justice

2

grind mighty slow. But they're set to grind fine as possible and Colorado saw him first."

Fagan scanned the writ in his hands again as he asked, "What if the murderous bastard beats this earlier Colorado case? You surely can't be fixing to set him *free*?"

Longarm shook his head and soothed, "If he beats our rap you get him back and I understand he's already been found guilty and condemned to death by hanging, here in Arkansas. So what have you all got to lose?"

"Time," sighed the Arkansas lawman, adding, "Every breath of life Frank Hungerford takes is one more breath than he deserves. You'll see what I mean when you meet the son of a bitch!"

That was as close as Fagan would allow himself to come to saying Longarm could have Colorado's prior want. He sent Longarm back to the cell block with a deputy to do the dirty job of unlocking the damned cell.

As the turnkey on duty was opening up, Longarm and the killer they'd sent him for had time to size one another up through the bars. They'd naturally heard of one another, but they'd never met before and neither was looking at what he'd expected in his mind's eye.

Hungerford saw Longarm about as described but hardly as ferocious in appearance as some newspaper accounts might lead one to expect. Longarm stood tall in his stovepipe army boots under a black-coffee Stetson he wore cavalry straight and telescoped High Plains style. In between he had on the three piece tobacco tweed suit current federal dress code required for court duty. The utilitarian but tailored grips of Longarm's double-action .44-40 peeked out from under the tail of his coat from its cross-draw holster on his left hip. Anyone but a fool could see he was a solid specimen of tall tanned whipcord and whalebone nobody but a fool would want to mess with.

Longarm was bemused to see the famous Frank Hungerford looked younger than his reputation as an old

3

pro. Albeit old pro was a contradiction in terms when one considered the life expectancy of a hired gun.

Hungerford looked more like a spoiled rich kid who'd never done a day of honest work. He likely hadn't. His yellow sheets said he'd busted out of a boys' reform school at the age of nine and the next time his name was recorded by the law he'd developed into a lethal sixteen-year-old gun hand.

He stood a tad shorter than Longarm in his three-inch Texas heels and while he had to be thirty pounds lighter he was built way softer. He showed how much common sense he had when he jeered through the bars, "I understand you eat cucumbers and perform other wonders, Longarm. But to tell the truth, you don't look like much to me and I wonder how tough you'd be without that sixgun and other lawmen backing you!"

Longarm sighed. "Might as well get this over with," he said as he shucked his hat and coat, asking the deputy who'd led him back there to hold them for him as he unbuckled his sixgun and then, lest anyone accuse him of cheating, fished out his vest pocket derringer for the turnkey to hold as well.

He didn't have to ask them to open up and let him in. They were downright delighted to do so. As Longarm stepped into the cell the barred door clanged shut behind him and the famous Frank Hungerford backed off.

Longarm asked in a wondering tone, "Where are you going, sweetheart? Don't you want this dance? Anyone can see it's you and me, with my guns and any back-up out in the corridor. So when do we get to see how good you are?"

The self-indulgent gun fighter protested, "I never said nothing about a fistfight, Longarm! It wouldn't be fair! You're way bigger than me!"

Longarm smiled thinly to reply, "Do tell? I never might have noticed if *somebody* around here hadn't speculated on

4

how good I was without my guns and back-up. Have you ever taken it in your head to make money? Or would you rather drop your jeans and bend over for the soap?"

The famous Frank Hungerford got red-faced and blubbery as he pleaded with the Fort Smith lawmen to save him from sodomy.

The deputy holding Longarm's guns pointed out he'd gotten himself in the fix with his mouth and suggested he get down in his knees.

But as famous Frank began to cry Longarm laughed and said, "We got us a train to catch and I feel sure Famous Frank would as soon suck me off in our Pullman compartment if he ain't ready to respect his elders."

Famous Frank allowed he'd only been teasing and so Longarm put his guns, hat and coat back on to take his prisoner out front to sign for him.

They had to give the squirt his own high-crowned black Stetson and a black leather bolero jacket from Propery because they were his.

Out front they found Marshal Fagan anxious to leave. There was more to it than Sunday being his day of rest. It was cloudy in the west and looked like rain before sundown. Fagan pointed at the Regulator Brand clock on the wall, observing, "Next train for Little Rock leaves here at three and she's going on two-twenty. You are headed back to Denver by way of Little Rock, ain't you?"

Longarm said, "Got to, if we mean to arrive by rail. You gents here in Fort Smith were behind the door when the railroad tracks were handed out."

Fagan murderously muttered, "Tell me about it" as he indicated where Longarm was to sign their daily log. Longarm didn't have to tell anyone in Fort Smith about it. They were still nursing the wounds left by the U.S. Army Engineer's survey of 1853.

Fort Smith, founded on the remains of a decommissioned military outpost, might have been the Omaha of the 35th parallel had an otherwise fine army engineer known more about the ways politicians juggled numbers.

As other survey parties found the going rougher, Lieutenant Amiel W. Whipple was delighted with his progress across the Indian Nation: high plains beyond and sensible mountains with plenty of passes, all the way out to Pueblo de Los Angeles on the Pacific.

His only mistake had been the honest cost estimates he'd turned in with his survey. Nobody had told him congressmen always voted in accord with the lowest estimate, even when they knew they were being slathered in snake oil. So they'd bought the snake oil estimates that would lead to the Credit Mobilier scandal and the railroad stock panic of '73 and the Union Pacific out of Omaha—leaving Fort Smith an afterthought on the railroad grid of the west.

But if getting in and out of Fort Smith by rail was a bother it still had any other current form of transportation beat. So when one of the Fort Smith lawmen suggested the stage line running directly north to K.C. Longarm shook his head to explain, "Appearances on the map are deceiving. Coach averages nine miles an hour. Railroads run forty an hour or more. Me and my traveling companion, here, will be transferring to a northbound out of Little Rock before the stage makes her far north as Fayetteville. So we'd better get cracking. I'd hate to have us miss our train on a rainy Sunday afternoon!"

Marshal Fagan cast a thoughtful glance at the soft-looking but deadly prisoner and decided, "I'm sending two men with you, far as the terminal. How come he ain't wearing irons?"

Longarm said, "Didn't bring 'em here from the terminal baggage room. I got 'em if we need 'em. But it's commencing to look as if old Frank and me will get along. Ain't that right, Frank?"

The subdued Hungerford said, "I ain't looking for trouble, Deputy Long."

Longarm turned back to Fagan to say, "There you go, Marshal. We don't need nobody to nursemaid us far as the terminal. We're both old enough to cross the street without nobody holding out little hands."

Fagan said, "I'm putting the two of you aboard that train safe and sound. What happens after you leave my jurisdiction won't be on my head."

Longarm didn't argue. He was in a hurry. He thought he was playing it smart, or leastways modest, by not protesting he preferred to work alone with good reason.

Wild Bill Hickok gunning his own deputy that time in Abilene was only one bad example of the mistakes that could happen when a man fighting for his life lost track of others on his side.

But what the hell, it would be less than an hour before he and his prisoner were on their way, leaving him free to blaze away at anybody he felt like. So Longarm and famous Frank were escorted to the nearby terminal across what had once been a military parade ground while, sure enough, little frogs or big rain drops commenced to hop around in the sun-baked dust all around.

They called one of Fagan's boy Grits and the other one answered to Sandy. Longarm was never going to get it straight in the time he would know them. It was coming down harder as the four of them stomped into the nigh-deserted waiting room, where an elderly colored woman seemed the only other passenger waiting on that three o'clock eastbound.

Longarm left his prisoner in the armed and dangerous care of Grits and Sandy while he went to the baggage counter to reclaim his overnight bag of saddle leather. He'd had no call to haul his saddle along on a legwork chore. He could see his overnighter on a shelf in the back. But when he waved his claim check at it the pimple-faced clerk told him only the baggage manager had the authority to hand it back.

Longarm allowed that was a hell of a way to run a railroad and asked where such a figure of authority might be found.

The kid suggested his boss might be with the station manager, around on the far side of the ticket window. Longarm strode out on the rear platform in search of the same. It was coming down harder, now. When he came to a door marked STATION MANAGER he found it locked. He knocked and knocked some more, muttering, "Where in hell might everybody *be* with a train coming in any minute?"

He was answered by the crackle of thunder, or what sounded like it if that had been thunder that morning at Shiloh and then Longarm was running back to the waiting room with his sixgun drawn.

As he dashed into the gunsmoke-filled waiting room he crabbed out of line with his back to the wall, calling out, "Grits? Sandy? You boys all right?"

There came no answer. Longarm was on one knee with his sixgun ready for anything as the smoke slowly cleared in eerie silence.

He spotted Grits or mayhaps Sandy spread-eagle on his back, smiling up at the pressed tin ceiling with bloody teeth. His pard lay face down but just as dead near the far door. There was no sign of that pimple-faced clerk, that elderly colored woman nor, of course, the famous Frank Hungerford.

So Longarm ran out front to fire three times at the rain clouds above.

Then, having sounded the universal call for others to come running, there was nothing he could do but stand there in the rain, getting soaked to the skin as he felt like a fool.

8

For they'd played him for a fool with one of the oldest dodges along the Owlhoot Trail, complete to the mock bravado at the jail to throw him off his guard, taking the famous Frank Hungerford for a moon calf when all the time he'd deserved to be famous as an old pro who'd just taught them all a thing or two about overconfidence.

And even as he stood there getting wet and feeling dumb he was only commencing to savvy what he was up against.

They found the baggage master's body with that of the station master and ticket clerk, behind that locked door, as Marshal Fagan was forming a posse to cross over into the Indian Territory after the muderous sons of bitches.

Longarm declined the invitation to ride with them. He hadn't brought his saddle and he somehow doubted anybody that slick would take such an obvious escape route.

Chapter 2

Judge Parker was literally mad as a wet hen by the time he met with Longarm in chambers at the courthouse built to resemble Mount Vernon. For first his church picnic had been rained out and then he'd arrived at home to be told of five murders and an escape the infernal newspapers were sure to descirbe as "daring."

After that Isaac C. Parker was older than Longarm but young for such a distinguished position. Reporters were forever confusing him with his longer-bearded spectral hangman. His Honor was a still-handsome man who trimmed his whiskers more like Buffalo Bill. As a former Ohio congressman who'd naturally sided with the Union, he was regarded with more than a little suspicion by the kith and kin of recent Confederate riders, red or white, who appeared before him and, the distaste being mutual, some of the wry remarks he made on passing judgement with no appeal tended to read unfortunately in print.

His Honor and Longarm went back a ways and viewed one another with a mutual respect tempered by honest differences as to how one addressed a fellow man about to die.

Longarm tended to feel sorry for those outlaws he was forced to kill. Mayhaps because he never killed them *per-*

sonally, Judge Parker was inclined to rub it in. Judge Dickerson up to Denver could get sardonic when he told a man found guilty what was about to happen to him. Longarm had sometimes wondered what those head doctors over to Vienna Town would make of that.

He was wondering what a doctor dealing in lunacy might make of the confusion of guilt and rage he was feeling, himself, as His Honor said he was surprised he hadn't borrowed horse and saddle to splash on over to the Indian Territory as it kept raining fire and salt.

Longarm explained, "I ain't one for going through the motions, your honor. I stayed in town to ask you for a federal arrest warrant. Papers I left Denver with only authorized me to transport an already caught son of a never-mind back to my own federal district. I'd like to leave here with murder warrants to serve on Hungerford and any number aiding and abetting the same."

The older man sat down at his desk in his soggy duds to reach in a drawer for the printed forms as he asked, "Then you really think that old colored woman as well as the youth posing as a baggage clerk were in on Hungerford's escape?"

Longarm nodded soberly and said, "Only way I can get it to work, your honor. I was a fool for turning my back on any prisoner with *his* yellow sheets, but he was still covered by two trained deputies. Grits had to have been gunned in the back by one whilst the other dropped Sandy the same way at the same time. Likely on cue. Where my deposition says the only other person in that waiting room struck me as an elderly colored woman I'm recording no more than appearances. She could have been a man disguised as a woman. I have to confess I never thought to go over and lift up her dress."

Even as he got busy with pen and ink on the printed forms, a jurist who'd had most everything evil appear be-

12

fore him mused, "So you'll be searching for Hungerford, a pimple-faced youth and a Negro of uncertain gender. Women shoot men in the back, too, you know. Where do you mean to start your search?"

Longarm said, "Indian Territory, same as Marshal Fagan, once it stops raining and I get some answers around here. I understand Hungerford was due to hang for gunning two of Fagan's deputies over in the Osage strip?"

Parker said, "He never told us what he was doing over there when they tried to get him to stop. He kept saying he wasn't there and hadn't done it. Never drygulch a rider from cover and use his body as bait for another back-shooting with Indian kids watching you from other cover. His lawyer tried to get him off by casting doubt on the word of wards of the U.S. government. Happens I know the Tallchief family as respected elite of the Osage Nation."

Longarm made a mental note of the name. He had no call to mention the times he'd been over in the Osage strip. He asked if Hungerford had stood trial with a court-appointed lawyer.

Blotting the ink on the arrest warrants the fastidious Judge Parker shook his head and replied, "Out of towner. Member of the Texas Bar as a matter of fact. But I allow any member of any local bar to appear in my federal court, as long as he behaves himself."

Longarm fished a damp notebook from his soggy suit and groped for a pencil stub in another pocket as he asked if they had a record of such a lawyer's name.

Isaac Parker proved what some said abut his steel trap mind to be true as he replied without hesitation, "W. R. Lovecraft, Wichita Falls on the Red River of the South. Blew in like a big wind in a white ten gallon hat with Van Dyke beard to match and seemed astounded I refused to grant bail to a man fleeing justice in other parts who'd murdered two federal deputies in cold blood."

13

As Longarm wrote all tht down His Honor added, "That was before he tried to play on any racial prejudice an Ohio man might harbor toward Indians who'd sided with the Union during the irregular warfare out this way."

Longarm felt no call to point out the Osage had likely sided with the north because the Cherokee had sided with the south. He found it more interesting a lawyer had come all the way from West Texas to defend a killer standing trial in Arkansas. Just getting there from West Texas could be daunting. Thanks to time out during the war and Reconstruction, Texas railroads had some catching up to do and . . .

"This big wind from Texas would have perforce arrived the hard way across the Indian Territory," Longarm exclaimed.

Handing the arrest warrant across the desk, Judge Parker grimaced and said, "I asked. He cited lawyer-client privilege. He was worth his salt, whoever hired him to defend young Hungerford."

"And Hungerford and his guns are hired by those who can afford to hire the best." Longarm nodded, folding the warrants and putting them in a dry inside pocket as he speculated, "Few full bloods or the half breeds and squatters to be found in the Indian Territory smoke Havana Perfectos or dine on caviar. Hungerford's yellow sheets put him on the payroll of more than one big mining, land or cattle outfit. So what if such an outfit out West Texas way sent Hungerford this way to do some dirty deed and after he got caught they hired a fancy lawyer to defend him and . . ."

Longarm grinned sheepishy and said, "I seem to be building a house of cards way in the middle of the air."

Judge Parker said, "I was just about to say that. I generally find some solid foundation before I lean the first two cards together."

Longarm nodded and said, "After I'm done with my

canvas here in Fort Smith I aim to poke about over in the Osage strip before I mosey on to Wichita Falls."

His Honor nodded approvingly and observed, "Step by step seems the way one gets anywhere. You'll be picking up a horse and saddle here, of course. Tell them out back I want them to issue you anything you need from our stable and tack room. Who do you intend to canvas? I thought you and Marshal Fagan's crew had canvassed all around the railroad terminal before I got back to town."

Longarm nodded and said, "We did. We failed to find anyone who'd seen anything. I mean to try harder. Could you all let me have say a Winchester '73 chambered for the same .44-40 rounds as this sixgun, You Honor?"

Parker nodded and said, "Have them issue you a couple of boxes of ammunition while they're at it. What are you getting at, even if you find some witness missed on the earlier try? We know Frank Hungerford, a white youth and a colored person of one sex or the other tore out of that waiting room into a summer squall. You need more?"

Longarm nodded and replied, "I'd like to know if it was just the three of them splashing about on foot or whether they had others waiting on them with ponies to ride off on or mayhaps a surrey with rain curtains down the sides. After that I'd like to hear which way they went. I'll be surprised to hear they bee-lined for West Texas by way of the Indian Territory, but I'm always getting in trouble when I overestimate the depths of the criminal mind. Hungerford could be dumb enough or scared enough to just streak across the kitchen floor like a cockroach."

The judge who'd tried and sentenced Famous Frank said, "You can't go wrong crediting Hungerford with cunning. Had we not had eye witnesses I doubt we'd have ever pinned a thing on him. We still don't know what he was up to in the Indian Territory and you just saw how cleverly he planned his escape, setting things up with his confederates before you ever got here."

Longarm had already figured it out. But a man who gloried in weighing the evidence step by step relentlessly opined, "Knowing you were on your way from Colorado, and knowing you'd be transporting him back there the same way, he had his confederates over at the terminal before the two of you left the lock-up. Knowing the time your train would back in for its run to Little Rock, they murdered thoe railroaders to lie in wait for you."

Longarm said, "Marshal Fagan sent their original plan out of kilter when he insisted on sending Grits and Sandy along. Had I arrived alone with Hungerford they'd have crossfired me in that waiting room. But when they saw it was two gun hands against three, the one playing baggage clerk thought fast on his feet and sent me on a fool's errand, making it two back-shooters against two unsuspecting victims. Otherwise, everything went just the way they'd planned."

"How?" asked the sharp thinking jurist, adding, "We had Hungerford under lock and key, awaiting the pleasures of old George Maledon. After all the hair-splitting sophistry of Lawyer Lovecraft I'd ordained his client was to have no private conversations with any visitors and I don't think he *had* any visitors those last few days when you were on your way from Denver, so . . ."

"So how could he have known I was coming and how could he have planned what he sure as shooting must have planned?" Longarm cut in with a wry expression.

Glancing at a nearby window he saw the rain was letting up a tad. He thanked His Honor for the warrants and such other courtesies as he'd be needing and left to run back to the lock-up, splashing some.

He didn't need to spend much time at the lock-up. A quarter hour later or less saw him striding into the beanery across the way, asking to see their manager.

The weary-looking cuss behind the counter said, "You're talking to him. If you're from the board of health we already caught the mouse that fussy old customer got so exited about."

Longarm introduced himself as federal law and allowed he'd try some of marble cake with black coffee as he eased on to a counter stool.

As the older man filled his order, Longarm told him, "Main reason I'm here is 'cause they just told me over to the lock-up you run trays of warm grub to those prisoners who can afford to pass on white bread and beans."

The beanery manager shrugged and said, "It ain't against the law. It's a free country and a man's entitled to eat as well as he can afford to, even when old George is fixing to hang him."

Longarm tried some of the marble cake, pronounced it swell and went on to explain, "Up Denver way, not long ago, an innocent waitress delivering take-out orders from an innocent Greek was used as a murder weapon by a sneak who slipped poison syrup aboard the breakfast tray she delivered to the intended victim. Poor cuss poured the poisoned syrup over his waffles himself. Ain't that a bitch?"

The Fort Smith beanery manager demanded, "Who's been poisoned by any grub we ever delivered anywhere to anyone?"

Longarm soothed, "Nobody. They just told me over to the lock-up you sent different help at different times with goodies for the sweet-toothed Frank Hungerford."

The man behind the counter brightened and said, "Oh, him? He ordered heaps of grub at all hours. That name he made up for himself sure fits him."

Longarm started to ask how the older man knew, or thought he knew, that Famous Frank Hungerford had invented his professional name. As soon as he considered how many other Hungerford's he'd ever heard of, he saw it might be a dumb question. But that wasn't one of the questions he had in mind at the moment. He explained, "I now

17

suspect he might have had sudden whims to order out so's he could pass messages back and forth, no doubt by written word. They told me at the lock-up you all serve grub on chinaware aboard a tin tray, with no paper napkins?"

When the man behind the counter said it was up to the customers to eat tidy or find their own damned wipe-offs Longarm said, "Best way in in that case would call for messages writ with grease pencils on china of the bigger plates. Neither your waiters nor the turnkeys idly viewing the proceedings would be likely to notice words scrawled on the *bottoms* of plates riding upright on tin trays, see?"

The older and more experienced hand at take-out orders shook his head and objected, "Dishwasher in the back would surely notice anything you wrote on either side of a fool plate he was *washing*!"

Longarm rinsed the cake in his mouth down, nodded, and said, "I was just fixing to go that way. Who but the one employee who takes in china, washes the same and hands it out as called for would be in better shape to serve as the conduit betwixt a prisoner ordering heaps of grub at odd times and say a customer seated right here on this stool, free to write anything he liked on the bottom of *his* plate?"

He set his fork down and soberly asked to have a word with their dish washer.

The man behind the counter said, "He ain't here right now. Lord knows where he went, just before noon and forcing me to put a mighty pissed off waitress to washing dishes in his stead! I know good help is hard to find. But I've a mind to fire him when or if he ever comes back!"

Longarm said, "He won't be coming back. What did he look like?"

The boss the mysterious dishwasher had deserted said, "Young squirt with limp rope-colored hair and a whole lot of pimples. Said his name was Billy Rom."

Longarm blinked and decided, "Rom. He gave the name of Rom, meaning Gypsy. He usually goes by the

18

name of the Tinker Kid, Tinker being the name of an Irish Gypsy clan! Might your Irish Gypsy dish washer have offered you any way to get in touch with him, here in Fort Smith?"

The man behind the counter said, "Sure. You didn't think I'd hire any hobo out of thin air, did you? Hold on, I got the address of the kid's boarding house here, somewheres."

Chapter 3

The widow Barnes, Zenobia Barnes, did not run a boarding house. But she'd fixed up quarters for hire above her carriage house and told the lawman flashing a badge at her he'd just missed young Billy Rom, who'd checked out that very morning.

She said her friends called her Zee and she was able to add the pimple-faced youth had left with his baggage in a delivery dray hauled by one mule and driven by a colored man Billy had called Algernon.

When she added Algernon seemed an odd name for a colored man Longarm replied, "It's an odd name for most anyone, Miss Zee. But now that I got my head screwed back on it could denote a want called Artistic Algernon Jackson, who deserted the Tenth Cav a spell back to go into the cattle business with a running iron. That's an illegal branding iron one can draw most any brand with, if he has the artistic skill. I'd never seen either of them in the flesh before they hornswaggled me in a railroad waiting room this afternoon. But two notorious West Texas wants and a fancy West Texas lawyer have commenced to add up. Could I take a look around the quarters you rented to the

21

Tinker Kid, Miss Zee? I know it's getting on towards supper time and all, but . . ."

"I dine alone whenever I please" she cut in, adding, "Follow me. I must admit you've aroused my curious nature!"

As he followed the shapely gal of say thirty-five across her well-kept back yard, past a whitewashed shithouse nobody was ever going to mention, Longarm noticed his own nature getting aroused. The long train he'd disenjoyed from Denver had involved hours of celibate sitting on ever-tingling seats of railroad plush, a mysterious substance that looked like velvet and felt like sandpaper.

The well-rounded widow Barnes was wearing a summerweight frock of beige pongee, another mysterious material. The rough wild silk rode cool on one's hide in warm Arkansas weather because the knots and snarls in the weave kept most of it clean off the same, letting one's sweat, or in a lady's case, one's *glow* escape through the loose weave, even as it hid the simple fact you were traipsing about nigh naked with mostly no more than the *shadows* of the flesh-colored pongee hiding any shame you might feel from the world.

Zenobia Barnes didn't seem to feel much shame as her pongee skirts swished behind her like the tail of a frisky palomino who might or might not be in heat.

Longarm warned himself not to study on such notions as he followed her into the carriage house and up a narrow flight of stairs to the quarters in what had once been a hay loft.

Neither the two stalls nor carriage space below had been in use for some time, judging by the clean smell.

Say what one cared to about decamping outlaws, the Tinker Kid had left no mess behind him to clean up, or mayhaps sifted through for clues.

Zenobia Barnes sighed and said, "He paid his rent on time and never had any late night guests, and you tell me he was some sort of outlaw?"

Longarm replied, "Not *some* sort of outlaw, Miss Zee.

He was, and is, a notorious cattle thief, wanted in more than one state for murder as well. Soon as I put the two descriptions together in my head the wanted fliers just popped out at me. The Tinker Kid and Artistic Algernon are known to have worked together on that new range opened in West Texas by the Comanche losing their buffalo war."

He saw she didn't follow him and explained, "Up to the late '70s the Staked Plains and Panhandle of West Texas was held against all comers by the Comanche Nation. Pound for pound the most dangerous horse Indians on the high plains."

She said, "I read the Sioux were wilder. Haven't the Sioux killed more white people than anyone else?"

Longarm shook his head and told her, "The Nakota, Dakota, Lakota or Sioux, depending on who you ask, only got down to serious fighting with our kind during the war, when Little Crow of the Santee Sioux saw fit to follow the war path with most of the Union Army otherwise occupied. The Comanche, distant kin to the Mexican Aztec, were killing white folk, or leastways Spaniards, before the Pilgrims landed at Plymouth Rock. They turned on the Anglo-Texans as soon as they had Anglo-Texans to turn on. The Texas Rangers bought out the entire stock of a bankrupt young gunsmith named Colt to deal with the Comanche and it was still a near thing. When they cashed in their chips *after* Little Big Horn they could brag on having killed more folk, red, white, black or brown, than all the other quill Indians combined."

She dimpled at him to tease, "I'm so happy for them. But you say others are raising cattle on their old hunting grounds, now?"

Longarm replied, "That's about the size of it. After their half-breed chief Quanah led the last hold-outs into Fort Sill in '75 the famous Captain Goodnight, who'd been playing tag with Comanche for a spell, moved his cattle operations back from Colorado to help himself to the Comanche stronghold of Palo Duro in the Texas Panhandle. Still running the same as the ever-expanding Old Home Ranch. Other big spreads have sprung up all across former Indian range out yonder. Outfit called the Matador Land and Cattle Company has been expanding even faster, backed by a Scots beef importing outfit. Understand Matado just bought a whole lot of Jingle Bob stock, too."

"Jingle what?" she laughed.

"Jingle Bob," he said. "Named for the ear marks of a big Pecos Valley outfit, fallen on hard times after an ill-advised range war. Ain't heard tell of any such nonsense in the Texas Panhandle, but that's the sort of trouble hired guns such as Frank Hungerford hire out for."

"Shall we go back to the house? It's getting dark out," she replied in the tone bored women use when changing subjects.

The view was a tad tougher to take in but if anything more tempting as he followed her frisky skirts back to her kitchen door through the gathering dusk. He was trying to figure a graceful way to phrase it when she turned to him in her dark kitchen to ask, "Do you think it wise to light the lamp? What if they come back? Do they really come back or is that just a cliche?"

He said, "Cliches get to be cliches by being true a heap of the time, Miss Zee. The birds I'm after ain't been gone but a few short hours and it's true crooks are prone to pussy foot back along their own footsteps as dumb as that may sound."

She asked how come.

He said, "Some head doctors think a guilty conscience can't let well enough alone. You ever read that novel, *Crime and Punishment* by that unpronounceable Russian? Crooks must think much the same all over. In *Crime and Punishment* this young cuss with delusions of intelligence kills an old pawn broker lady and gets away clean with

24

some pocket jingle. But he can't take the suspense of waiting for a knock on his door. So he goes to this Russian lawman with advice on how to solve the murder."

She said, "But didn't he *know* who'd committed the murder, Deputy Long?"

He said, "My friends call me Custis. Sure he knew who dunnit. It was him. He thought he was tricking the lawman into telling him how much they had on him. But of course they'd never even considered him before he came to them with all that helpful advice. I reckon you can see for yourself how the story ends."

She said, "Land's sakes that *was* returning to the scene of the crime. Are you suggesting those boys might come back tonight to see . . . what?"

He said, "To see if we have the place staked out. If they don't see anybody watching for 'em they'll figure nobody back tracked those dirty dishes I told you about. So with your permit I'd like to watch out back from higher up. Might you have a top story window offering a view of the alley behind yonder carriage house, Miss Zee?"

She allowed she surely did and added it was all so thrilling.

That was what folk called a stake-out before they'd sat through one or more. Thrilling.

She took him by one hand lest he bump into things in the dark and led him out in her hall and up her stairs through some confusion until they were in a back bedroom with a rain-splattered rear window letting in enough light for her to let go. As he moved over to the window she asked if he could see down into the alley.

He replied, "Enough to make out anybody pussy footing along the same, Miss Zee. Do you mind if I draw these lace curtains across the glass? Glancing up at a blacked out window is inclined to make one wonder what such darkness might conceal."

She told him to go ahead. As he moved the open-weave

white lace in place he added, "We know better when we study on it. But blank whiteness in an unlit window tends to blind us to the window being there. Is it all right with you if I shift this chair from this vanity to this window?"

She told him to make himself at home and added she was going back down to the kitchen to whip them up a cold supper, being it had been hot and muggy all afternoon in any case.

He didn't argue. He hadn't noticed until she mentioned it how that marble cake he'd had earlier no longer seemed to be with him.

He was dying for a smoke as well. He was sure he could cup a palmed cheroot well enough to keep any sneaks in yonder alley from spotting the ruby glow through those curtains. He was sure nobody was about to come sneaking along yonder alley. But the room smelled of bath powder and lilac water, not three-for-a-nickel tobacco, and he owed the lady of the house something for wasting time up here at her expense.

The famous Frank Hungerford and his pals were pros. They'd know better than to hang about in Fort Smith after getting away clean in that summer squall. The gal down in the kitchen had *told* him they'd driven off in a horse drawn dray. Before the rain. Before the gunplay at the terminal. A canvas, all around, had failed to turn up any witness who could say which way the three of them might have driven. Following wheel ruts along public thoroughfares got you nowhere. Any sign they'd left cutting across less traveled ground had been smoothed over by all that rain by now. If they weren't long gone they were fixing to come in any minute and give themselves up. Because they'd just never meant to get away.

If they'd gotten away, what in thunder was he doing there, staring out at nothing much whilst hither and yon a distant lamp winked on amid the bewilderment of dark shadows.

"I'll tell you what you're doing here, old son," the voice of old Billy Vail back in Denver seemed to whisper from the backstage of his mind. "You're staying here and making certain because when you get back to Denver you know I'm going to ask if you covered every bet. Ain't that a bitch?"

It was. There was nothing he could do about it. As in the case of a soldier pulling night picket along a quiet sector he had to ignore the dead certainty he was wasting his time because any old soldier could tell you such certainty could lead to disaster.

The widow woman came back, bearing a tray piled high with potato salad and sandwiches with cool buttermilk from her ice box. In the dimmer light her oval face framed by her dark upswept hair made her look like a pretty teenager. He couldn't help wondering if that had been her real reason for suggesting they find their way in the dark to wherever they might be headed.

She set the tray on her vanity long enough to improvize a spot for it on a stool she dragooned as a bitty table between them as she slid another chair in place opposite his, asking along the way if he'd seen anything out back.

He'd just said, "Not hardly," when someone stuck a match in another window across the alley. As the gal holding it applied it to a candle tip he could see they were looking into another bedroom window. The gal who seemed to want some light on the subject was naked as a jay.

The range was about a tough pistol shot or say fifty yards. So it was uncertain just how pretty she might be, up close. She sure looked mighty tempting at fifty yards and anyone could see she was red-headed all over.

The brunette trying to feed him with more dignity sniffed, "Serving wench. From some outlandish place like Pomerania or Poland. They don't believe in window shades there, wherever it might be. Have you tried this liverwurst on rye, yet?"

27

He said, "I have. It's swell and ain't this egg mayonnaise I taste in your potato salad?"

She modestly admitted she'd bought it ready made at a High Dutch delicatessen, adding, "Since the price of ice has come down to where so many shops are using crushed ice . . . Don't look out the window, Custis!"

He said, "I got to, Miss Zee. I ain't watching yon serving wench with that . . . whatever. I got to keep an eye on the alley and I understand we owe such modern wonders to Mister Armour's new refrigerated box cars. Being they have to shovel crushed ice into all those hollows before they load the sides of beef aboard, most every meat packing town has one or more ice plants, now."

"Custis! Don't you dare watch that wicked thing!" she moaned.

He said, "Aw, you can't see all that much at this range. Even if you could there's not much any man could do for her that she don't seem to have a firm grip on. Them scientific ice plants they use now, instead of a limited supply of stored up winter ice, freeze branch water sort of tricky by pumping ammonia into expansion chambers in ways that sort of elude me."

She asked, "What do you make that . . . object to be?" asked Zee, adding in a sort of breathless way, "I can't make it out from here. It *looks* like a . . . never mind."

He said, "You call it a dildo, Miss Zee. They are sold in the sort of shops dispensing other rubber objects one does not mention in mixed company, along with French post cards and books with plain brown paper covers. Are you saying this is the first time yonder redhead has ever put on such a show?"

She flustered, "Maybe now and again. I usually don't spend this much time staring out my own bedroom window. Are you trying to tell me girls go out and *buy* such . . . scientific wonders?"

He answered, "I understand they're closer to the real thing than say a carrot or a cucumber."

She got up and moved over to stand against the bedroom wall with her back to him as she sighed, "Nothing is anything like the real thing. As many a woman in my position has discovered the hard way!"

So Longarm set the tray on the sill and rose to join her against the wall, gently turning her to face him as he wordlessly allowed her to feel it hard.

And from the way she responded they could both tell it was time they got out of such a ridiculous position.

On their fool feet—when there was a perfectly sound feather bed just a few steps away.

Chapter 4

As they lay entwined atop the rumpled bedding, sharing a smoke in the nude, Zee insisted he confess he'd been planning all along to seduce her. So he did and she said she was glad. It wasn't true, of course, but they both felt he owed her the common courtesy.

For as an older soldier had once confided to a young and horny Private Long, a military secret of the war betwixt the sexes was that women were the ones who'd mastered the arts of seduction, one facet calling for the women to never, ever admit this.

But the older soldier's words of wisdom had proven true every time Longarm had considered who was seducing whom. For short of forceable rape there was no way on earth a mere mortal man was about to have his way with a woman who wasn't interested in him. He could shower her with gifts and be dismissed as a fool who thought he could buy her love. He could fight duels over her and be written off as a suicidal show-off and the same applied to walking picket fences for her. Nothing a man could do or say if she didn't want him would ever get her to want him.

On the other hand, when the sweet little things *were* interested in a man, hardly anything he could come up

31

with was likely to help him escape the beating he was in for. It was barely *possible* to change a gal's plans for one's fate-way-nicer-than-death by pissing her off with an ill-chosen word or action. Assuring her your wife didn't understand you was one good example whilst farting on a porch swing was another. But as Longarm had just proven, a man who just let the little lady bob and weave until she caught you had it all over smooth-talking fans of the late Casanova, who'd been a fool librarian with a vivid imagination to begin with.

The older boys around a pool hall could see right through the just plain impossible brags of the lonesome liar and old Casanova had tried to sell some whoppers in his so-called confessions.

Having established in her own mind she was a poor weak-willed widow woman overwhelmed by a Casanova, Zenobia Barnes was proving herself a gal with a vivid imagination as well. More comfortable now with the subject of self-abuse, seeing he'd abused her with something wilder than a carrot, old Zee wanted Longarm to tell him more about those naughty shops that sold naughty naughties.

Snuggling her slighty over-ripe charms closer, Longarm allowed most of such trade was aimed at menfolk. He said, "I ain't sure why, but it seems to be true that men get more exited over dirty pictures whilst ladies are inclined to dildo themselves whilst reading a bad book. Nature gives you all the edge when it comes to love toys. Gals seem to be able to pleasure themselves with broomsticks, candlesticks, walkingsticks and such, whilst there hardly seems anything that can substitute for a ring dang doo."

"A ring dang what?" she coyly asked.

So Longarm set the cheroot aside, took the matter in hand and softly sang as he rocked the little man in the boat . . .

When I was young and in my teens

32

I met this gal from New Orleans,
And she was young, and pretty, too,
And had what she called her ring dang doo.

Zee said, "Oh," as she thrust her ring dang doo higher.

Longarm sang on . . .

She took me down to her father's cellar,
She told me I was a nice young feller.
She served me wine and whisky, too,
And let me play, with her ring dang doo!

She laughed but pleaded, "Stop it, the neighbors might hear you!"

So he stopped and she moaned, "I didn't meant to stop playing with my ring dang doo, you fool!"

So he made her come with his love-slicked fingers, it didn't take long, and then she rolled off the bed to scamper bare-ass down to her kitchen and return with a whole trug basket of somewhat phallic objects.

Longarm was game for anything that didn't hurt and Zee settled in the end on his treating her to uncooked corn on the cob lubricated with mayonnaise and moving in and out with spiral motions whilst, lest Longarm feel left out, she gave him an enthusiastic French lesson.

"I fear you've ruined my ring dang doo for life!" she lewdly laughed when they'd both climaxed in mingled ecstasy and dismay.

He suggested they stick to old-fashioned ways if they ever felt up to trying again.

She sighed and decided, "A she-salmon must feel like this after she's swum through all those rapids, spilled her guts and just lies there in the shallows, wondering what all the fuss was about! How can such lust for ever-more-down-and-dirty just fade away like smoke once we've made it up the rapids, Custis?"

He said, "Evolution. Professor Darwin explains how we evolved to move heaven and earth to get down and dirty, then evolved to lose the urge so's we can get on with life.

Think how little would get done if nobody ever stopped humping once they got started and that reminds me—I'd better have another look out the window."

Zee joined him there as they both peered out to see that redhead had blown out her candle or just lost interest. Zee whispered, "Land's sake! I'd forgotten the reasons we came up here to begin with! What if those outlaws took advantage of you whilst you were taking advantage of me all that time?"

Longarm led her back to bed, observing, "If nobody spotted a stake-out the Tinker Kid should think nobody traced him here from that beanery. If they weren't worried about that they never came by to see if there might be a stake-out. In either event the question before the house is my next best move. After I screw you some more, I mean."

She begged for mercy and asked what else he'd had in mind just now.

Settling back on the bed with her, Longarm explained, "The escaped federal prisoner I'm more serious about is a gun for hire. He kills for cash on the barrel head. So when those Fort Smith deputies spotted him over in the Osage strip he must have been there to kill somebody."

"Then you think that's the best place to hunt for them?" she asked.

He said, "Not once you study on it. Hungerford might or might not have finished his chores there before those deputies spotted him. Even if he hadn't, he knows that's the first neck of the woods Fagan and his Fort Smith crew will concentrate on. On the other hand the Tinker Kid and Artistic Algernon have been active of late in West Texas and somebody richer sent a West Texas lawyer in before them. Leaving more than a hint of West Texas chaparral in the air."

"You suspect some West Texas big shot set out to free Frank Hungerford with a view to hiring his gun?" she asked.

34

He nodded and caressed her pleasantly plump charms as he replied in a bemused tone, "Might be easier to fathom than even an important Osage slated for execution. Range wars are harder to conceal than tribal in-fighting and Fagan's riders know more than me about such matters. I got a name and address to go with Wichita Falls. Lawyer Lovecraft is a paid-up member of the Texas Bar Association, with clients I might manage to eliminate as suspects."

She asked why he wanted to eliminate suspects.

He said, "That's how come my boss calls it a process of eliminating. You eliminate all the suspects you can and the ones left are more than likely guilty. I can already think of a lot of rich cattle barons who'd have no use for a hired gun."

Musing aloud half to himself, the experienced hand in such matters marveled, "It sure beats all how some stockmen, as if they didn't have enough on their plate what with hoof-and-mouth, larkspur poisoning, dry water holes and fickle beef prices think it wise to declare war on the neighbors."

He groped for that cheroot he'd snuffed earlier as he went on, "Old Captain Goodnight has ever been content to fight it out with Indians and other natural perils of the plains. He's never given another stockman a hard time. Same goes for the late lamented J.W. Iliff who grazed ninety miles of range along the South Platte and never let a poorer neighbor go hungry. When he died the *Cheyenne Leader* described him as the best as well as squarest cattleman who ever forked a bronc. *The Rocky Mountain News* described him as 'Cattle King Of The Plains' and both papers got no argument. Yet neither J.W. nor any of his many riders ever shot a dirty look at anybody large or small."

Zee suggested, "Maybe he was simply mild-natured. It could happen."

Longarm said, "You'd hardly call old Shanghai Pierce down Texas way mild-mannered. Stands six foot five with

35

ferocious whiskers and spur rowls bigger than silver dollars, old rooting tooting Shanghai Pierce grazes over a million acres of range on his well-named Rancho Grande and yet, to date, has never had a feud with anybody!"

He got the cheroot going, it only tasted terrible at first, and went on to observe, "Sensible men don't fight over public land that the Good Lord made so much of, out our way. You take Colonel Richard King down San Gertrudes way, for instance."

"Do I have to?" Zee sighed.

But Longarm was wound up and insisted, "Did he hire paid assassins when he gave up steamboating to claim the biggest spread in the west near the mouth of the Rio Grande? He hired three hundred Mex *vaqueros*. They were enough to cope with brush fires, floods, stock thieves and such to where, this very night, they say the King Ranch grazes sixty or seventy thousand cows, eleven thousand horse, eight thousand goats, seven thousand sheep and Lord knows how many pigs and chickens without making faces at anyone else. Range wars have ruined every would-be cattle baron engaged in one. From the DeWitt County War of the '60s to the Lincoln County War of the '70s. With a heap of innocents hurt as well. So all in all I'd best beeline for Wichita Falls and points west and see if I might nip another range war in the bud as I round up at least three troublemakers attracted to such noise, if not already on somebody's payroll out yonder."

She quietly asked when he might be leaving. When he told her she sighed and said, "Then do me wrong some more but this time take it easy, will you?"

So he tried. She sighed in contentment and they even caught a few winks, followed by breakfast in bed and a morning quickie that left Zee weeping into a pillow as he got dressed and shut the door softly after himself as he left. There was no easier way to leave a lover, when you had to leave a lover.

When he reached the courthouse Longarm found Marshal Fagan and his posse had turned back from a pointless ride through pounding rain and commenced to track the more modern way by telegraph. A wire from the Osage Police in Tulsa Town saved Longarm further guilt about not being able to cover widely seperated bases at the same time.

Frank Hungerford's ill-advised foray into country where he'd stood out like a sore thumb had likely been inspired by the mortification of a rich skirt-chasing Kansan from Coffeeville, who'd had words at an Osage dance he'd never been invited to and muttered the dire threats of a rich drunk as they were running him out of town. Hungerford was known to have passed through Kansas on the run from that original Colorado warrant. He'd likely detoured into the Indian Territory on retainer from the poor loser. Marshal Fagan said he'd be working that angle with the Federal District of Eastern Kansas.

Longarm advised Fagan of his plans to interview Lawyer Lovercraft when he got to Wichita Falls. Fagan said, "Save your breath. Lovercraft is one oily son of a bitch who, unfortunately, has all the dirty parts of the U.S. Constitution committed to memory. We already *tried* to get him to tell us who retained him to defend Hungerford. He pointed out and Judge Parker was forced to agree through gritted teeth, no lawyer is required by law to reveal toad squat about a client when said client may be neither wanted nor *known* to courts disputing his right to appear before it. He said he'd come to defend Frank Hungerford and who might or might not pay his confidential retainers had no bearing on the case."

Longarm couldn't prove his educated guess about an unethical lawyer setting up that dodge involving messages written on the bottom of plates and he didn't want to start gossip in a small town about Zenobia Barnes. So he only suggested, "Cattle baron saving gun waddies from the

37

hangman to give his neighbors a hard time should be the sort of neighbor you see in court a heap. Don't you reckon such a sweet-natured individual ought to have a lawyer of record listed with more than one court clerk?"

The Fort Smith Federal Marshal smiled thinly and allowed he did, adding, "You're saying there's a range war fixing to bust out over yonder? How come things still seem so peaceful up this side of the Goodnight trail? There's more grass than any herd could eat across the Staked Plains and up into the Texas panhandle."

Longarm said, "You're talking common sense. There's never enough range nor room on this Good Earth for a born bully."

He went on to repeat his observations about the bigger more successful cattle barons avoiding trouble by simply acting neighborly. Marshal Fagan went along with most he said but objected, "Hold on. I never hears Shanghai Pierce described as no pussy cat. Wasn't he mixed up in that De-Witt County War?"

Longarm shrugged and said, "He was there, riding younger for others and hard to ignore at six foot five. But I've won bar bets off newspaper men who searched their newspaper morgues in vain for a single instance of Shanghai Pierce harming a hair on anybody's head. They call him Shanghai because of the way he struts around like a flashy Shanghai rooster in his monstrous spurs. But he ain't a fighting cock. He's a savvy businessman who worked himself up from cowboy to cattle baron without making enemies he didn't need. So I'm looking for a cattle baron who may or may not look as flashy, but feels he needs to have enemies."

Fagan nodded and said, "Well, let's go out back and fix you up with the horse, saddle and saddle gun His Honor mentioned earlier."

Longarm said, "That was then. Before I knew how far I

had to ride in quest of Famous Frank Hungerford and the fool who busted him out to add him to the payroll."

Fagan frowned thoughtfully and asked, "What am I missing? Do you aim to get from here to West Texas on *foot*?"

Longarm nodded and said, "Most of the ways. I'll need horseflesh to get around once I get there. But they don't allow you to lead a horse aboard a Pullman car."

Fagan laughed at the picture and asked, "You expect to take the *train*?"

To which Longarm could only reply, "I do, and with any luck I might beat Hungerford and his pals to Lawyer Lovecraft. If they beeline west through the Indian Territory the old-fashioned way."

Chapter 5

Modern manners were mostly a matter of mind-set. The advances of the Industrial Revolution tended to leave old-fashioned minds behind and a heap of the human race still made travel plans based on the ways folk had gotten around before the dawn of history.

Men still young enough to pester women could remember when there was no faster way to travel overland than Julius Caesar had enjoyed, or mayhaps Queen Elizabeth if you considered the invention of the coach over in Hungaria an improvement. So men still young enough to pester women still thought in terms of a twelve miles a day cattle drive or at best the ninety miles a worn-out Pony Express or Mongol dispatch rider might manage.

Yet the Iron Horse poked along at twenty miles an hour running *local* and averaged forty or fifty miles an hour along express runs. (There'd been runs for the record at the astounding speed of a mile a minute but only along recently inspected tracks, and Longarm took that yarn about one locomotive cranked up to a hundred miles an hour with a grain of salt.)

The catch, of course, was the way the railroads of the

land had been laid out, with more tracks leading to places of more interest.

Thanks to the war, Reconstruction and Indian troubles, nobody had been interested until recently in laying tracks across much of West Texas and that, more than Ned Buntline's romantic twaddle about modern knights on paint ponies, had led to the legendary cattle drives of recent memory, with some few still going on along the newly surveyed Ogallalah Trail serving the Texas panhandle as it's north-bound outlet.

In sum, a pilgrim traveling south of the Arkansas by rail had some poring over maps and time tables to accomplish and he still had to free his mind of the old superstition that the shortest distance between two points was a straight line. That didn't apply when one averaged three miles an hour by saddle bronc, nine miles an hour by coach, or forty miles an hour by rail.

So the route Longarm finally worked out seemed to take him all over Robin Hood's barn but promised to get him there faster than anybody about to cut across the Indian Territory with horsepower.

Fort Worth, a hundred miles short of his goal, was the best they could do for him by rail. But the mail coach from Fort Worth to Wichita Falls got him there overnight to dismount travel sore and dusty with his one bag and expense account to work with.

Wichita Falls was the seat of Wichita County, named for the modest stream that fell some before it met up with the Red River of the South just to the north. The country to the west was wilder. There was nothing in the way of public transportation and you had to manage another hundred miles to say you were in the panhandle. Texas was a caution for elbow room. The notion anybody might try to hog such range sounded comic opera until you considered how long Forever would be. For unlike the way folk died on the stage in comic operas, they were dead forever when they died in a range war.

The day being young, even if Longarm felt he was getting old after that all-night coach ride, he checked into a middle class hotel on their main street and opened his overnighter to lay out clean underwear before he stripped and had a whore's bath at the corner washstand. In summertime south of the Arkansas he'd naturally switched from that tweed suit to broken-in blue denim Miss Lemonade Lucy Hayes in Washington need never concern her pretty prudish head about. But even dressed way lighter a man sweated some down that way at that time of the year.

Cleaned up but not bothering to shave that morning, Longarm beat as much dust as he could out of his denim jeans and jacket to put them on over a fresh work shirt and clean underwear. Then he strapped on his .44-40, tucked his derringer and attached pocket watch in a jacket pocket and sallied forth into the sun dazzle of a cloudless West Texas workday.

First things coming first and lawyers keeping the same hours as slugabed bankers, Longarm spent some time at a livery up the street at the fine-honed skills of horse trading. The old bandit with more horse-flesh than common sense on his hands seemed to feel Longarm had to be a royal prince touring the American west incognito. When he offered to throw in a battered stock saddle with an elderly chestnut barb for a hundred dollars Longarm laughed and said, "That critter is a gelding. How could I ever marry a sexless horse to have and to hold 'til death us did part? Army officers are paying two hundred for sixteen-hand cavalry chargers this summer, with Indian trouble in mind. That chestnut has to stand on tippy-hoof to make fourteen hands and he's built like a barrel besides!"

The bewhiskered horse trader snorted, "All barbs are short of spine by one vertebra. That's how come they can turn on a dime at full gallop and old Buscadero, here, is an experienced cutting horse!"

Longarm replied, "I believe you. He's old enough to be experienced at most anything but fornication, poor old nut-less thing. I ain't out to cut no cows. Need to sit down some as I travel cross country. This hang-dog horse might or might not move faster than I can manage in a rocking chair so I'll give you twenty for him, saddle and all."

The horse trader gasped as if he'd been kneed in the groin and told Longarm to go play marbles with the other little kids, adding, "I am open for *business*, not bullshit. I ain't coming down below seventy-five!"

They finally settled on an even fifty. Longarm really wanted such a frisky-looking mount and the saddle alone was worth ten and looked to be comfortable as well as broken in past pretty.

So they spit on their palms and shook on the deal and Longarm rode old Buscadero, meaning "Hunter" when applied to a horse, back to his hotel. He tipped the hotel stable hands to take good care of the brute for the time being.

His next stop was a closed pawn shop, where he picked up a Winchester '66 Yellowboy, a cheaper but fair substitute for the Model '73 he'd left in Denver. Named for its brass instead of steel receiver, the Yellowboy, like the Henry it was descended from, would still throw the same slugs his sixgun was chambered for fast as he cared to pump the lever. The pawn shop threw in the leather saddle boot Longarm needed for the rifle for an extra fifty cents. Like the saddle it was fixing to ride with, it was still ser-viceable but broken in past pretty.

He picked up two boxes of S&W .44-40 rounds, fifty to a box, at a handy hardware store. Then he carried every-thing back to his hotel and bet the upstairs maid she wouldn't be able to wake him up around one that afternoon.

After she'd put the bet he'd lost in an apron pocket

meant for such transactions Longarm stripped again and flopped across the bed under a single cotton sheet. He felt certain there had never been a softer bed nor silkier sheets created by human hands and then he seemed to be chasing a chestnut mare across a field of lavender with a raging hard-on, naked as a jay and hoping nobody was watching. Because he knew what they said about stable boys who set out to mount mares.

To begin with it seemed an exercise in futility and after that it was silly. So he stopped chasing that mare in heat across a field of lavender but she wouldn't stop shaking his shoulder.

So he opened his eyes and said "Howdy. What time is it?" to the no longer young upstairs maid who'd treated herself to lavender toilet water recently.

She said, "One o'clock. You said to wake you then, remember?"

Longarm muttered, "I must have been out of my mind and what the hey, lawyers stay open later than bankers, don't they?"

Then he thanked the middle aged drab who smelled so nice and raised himself up on one elbow, inspiring her to flee the room and allow him to get up and put himself back together, taking time to shave at the wash stand, that time.

Then he unpacked his officious three piece suit to pay a call looking officious on a shady lawyer.

But when he got to Lovecraft's office around quarter to two a mousy stenographer, law clerk or whatever told him her boss was over in the panhandle on business and she couldn't say when he might be back. When she added nobody around there ever told her anything Longarm believed her. Had she known her onions she'd have never said where her boss might be. "He's in conference" had been invented to tell visitors in a nice way it was none of their blamed business where the son of a bitch might be.

Knowing that returning with a search warrant was only

45

going to alert Lovecraft, Longarm decided to try her another way. He mosied over to the nearest bank, betting Lovecraft would have noticed how handy to his office it was and, sure enough, when another mouse led Longarm back to a private office the white-haired branch manager in an undertaker's suit eyed Longarm's badge and I.D. thoughtfully and grudgingly allowed W.R. Lovecraft, Attorney-at-Law, did indeed have a savings and checking account with them.

But when Longarm explained where he wanted to go from there the banker drew himself up like a queen who'd just been patted on the ass to say, as if reading letters written in stone, "Stockman's Savings and Loan does not divulge such information, Deputy Long."

When Longarm asked, "What if I come back with a search warrant?" the insulted queen sniffed, "You'll never make it back from the courthouse in time if you want to try. His Honor is a personal friend of mine and we close for the day at three."

Longarm sighed, rose to his considerable height and managed not to say, "Adios, Motherfucker!" as he thanked the same for his time through gritted teeth. His mother had always said you caught more flies with honey than with vinegar. His mother had never been west of the Big Muddy. But she's likely been right.

It wasn't getting any cooler as he stood out front in tobacco tweed with the white-hot sun glaring down from a cobalt sky. So he headed for the shade of an ice cream parlor awning across the way.

As he sank down out front in a wire chair at a bitty marble topped table he told the amused-looking teenager waiting tables, "By Gum. I *did* make it across that frying pan alive. But I sure need something cold inside me, now. Might you have some of that ice cream with no cream in it, miss?"

She asked, "You mean *sorbet*, sir?"

He said, "Yep, that too. I read where the ancient Persians invented it and that's how come it has such an odd name."

"We sell sorbet in three flavors, cherry, strawberry and lime for five cents a bowl," she cut in.

He smiled sheepishly and said, "Make mine lime, then. I know nobody cares where flavor ice comes from. I suspect I may be sun-stroked."

She left him there to work it out as she ducked inside to fill his order. Longarm reached for a smoke, decided not to and muttered, "You should have caught more sleep and less sun. Starting to flutter with your idle hands and you're running off at the mouth. There's no call to tell everybody how dumb you are. It's easier to just let 'em find out for themselves!"

The teenager came back with a bowl of emerald green delight and just as he was savoring the first spoonful he saw that mouse who'd led him back to see the old queen on her way to somewhere's else with a big envelope. As she crossed the same street, albeit not in line with the awning he was shaded by, Longarm rose and hailed her with a wave of his hat. But she said she was too busy to join him and tore on up the street with her banking chores.

So he sat back down, finished the lime sorbet and told the teenager he'd try their strawberry, next.

As he worked on that bowl he began to see how the young waitress got to look so cool on such a hot afternoon. Messing around with ice and ice cream was cooling even when you didn't eat much of it. He suspected they had a cold room in the back lined with frost-covered pipes filled with running brine colder than fresh water froze. As in the case of the Iron Horse, men just about right for pestering women could recall summers when the only ice to be had was the natural product of frozen-over northern lakes, cut into flat cakes and stored betwixt layers of sawdust in insulated ice houses. Thomas Jefferson had managed to serve

47

ice cream late as August. But it had been an expensive untidy proposition before not one but half a dozen ways to cool air and freeze water had popped into as many heads in recent times. They all involved the same scientific notion that any gas cooled down as it expanded. So when you packed gas tight as hell in what they called a heat exchanger and let it cool natural down to the temperature of the day, it got cold as hell expanding into bigger pipes and after that there were too many ways to run an ice house or cold storage plant to shake a stick at. So now they could serve ice box ice, iced tea, ice cream and such at prices the common folk could afford, and Longarm was pleased as punch about that on a West Texas afternoon.

So he was enjoying a smoke as he dawdled over some lime sorbet he's rotated back to when that same mouse from the bank across the way came back from wherever she'd been, minus her load and looking as if she was fixing to drop as she tottered by with the straw boater pinned to her hair at a cockeyed angle and gasping for breath.

Longarm jumped to his feet, ran out on the dazzle and grabbed her from behind by both elbows, saying, "We'd better set you down in some shade and cool off your innards before you explode."

She weakly gasped, "Unhand me, sir! What is the meaning of this?" as she let him steer her to his table under the awning, set her down across from him, and tell the startled waitress they needed more lime sorbet on the double.

The teenager proved she knew a thing or two about sun stroke when she brought a cup of tea and a damp towel from the kitchen on the same tray with the dangerous refreshment Longarm had ordered.

"Where am I? What's going on? Give me back my hat!" the mouse from the bank let fly, as the waitress cooled her brow and Longarm got some tea with plenty of sugar into her.

As she recovered her senses she began to look less like

a mouse and more like a maiden in distress. Sort of pretty at second glance if you didn't mind gals who didn't stand out in a crowd.

She looked prettier when she dimpled up at Longarm to say, "Oh, I remember you! You're that lawman I took in to see Mister Gilchrist! I seem to be sitting out front of the ice cream parlor across the street with you. How did that happen?"

Longarm said, "First you'll eat your sorbet before it melts. Then we'll talk."

Chapter 6

Cooled down enough to taste her sorbet she pronounced it heavenly and said her name was Charity, Charity Barnes. It wasn't easy, but Longarm managed not to observe Charity seemed a funny name for anyone working in a bank. He wanted her on his side, not defending her name.

After he'd told her who *he* was he found she seemed interested in how the ancient Persians had invented sorbet the hard way, running snow off the mountains in baskets packed by barefoot slaves. She never told him to shut up when he added, "They say the Emperor Nero heard of the practice and sent his own runners up to his own mountains and that's how Italian Ice got invented. I'm still working on the difference."

The waitress lounging in the doorway where a draft was blowing piped up, "Italian Ice is crushed ice with flavors poured over it. Sorbet has the flavoring in the water as it freezes whilst being churned to keep it smooth like ice cream."

Charity said, "My, this has all been so educational! But I'd better get back to my desk before Mister Gilchrist misses me!"

Longarm said, "He won't. Saw him leaving as I was trying the strawberry sorbet, earlier. I never invited him over for any. He didn't look like he'd want any."

Charity dimpled and confided, "We girls call him Big-Chief-Walk-On-Water behind his back. I still have to dismiss the other help and lock up across the way by five, though."

He said he'd thought banks closed at three.

She explained how banks closed to the public still had chores to tend to behind locked doors and he began to know how that waitress likely enjoyed lectures on the shit she served all day.

Longarm knew as much or more about banking as any banking gal young as Charity. Bank examination was the chore he had in mind. But like it or not and hard as it was, you caught more flies with honey than with vinegar and got more out of the duller-witted folk you met up with by acting even dumber.

He'd often wondered why they didn't teach such facts of nature in schools of higher learning. He'd often felt embarrassed for educated dudes sent out in the field on scientific chores as they lectured trail guides red or white on the flora, fauna and geology all around. Indians who could sniff a horse apple and tell you whether a red or white man had been feeding it never let on they knew anything for certain. The Lakota even dismissed the Great Spirit invented by missionaries as the *Wakan Tanka* or big mystery. They didn't see how anyone or anything half that important might feel obliged to explain who or what he, she or it might be to any human being.

Charity snapped him out of his reverie by finishing her sorbet, downing her spoon, and declaring she had to get back to work.

Longarm rose with her, slapping a silver dollar down on the marble to cover all possible bets with a tip as he declared he was fixing to assure she made it safe and sound.

She didn't see fit to argue. So they headed across arm in

arm as behind them their waitress started to call out, grinned like a mean little kid and made change for the till from her earlier tips.

They'd established, eating sorbet, that Charity dwelt alone over by the falls. Sensing her reluctance as they got to the locked doors of her bank, knowing she felt awkward about inviting him in after closing time with all that money in the vaults and all the other help likely to smirk, Longarm let out more line lest she throw the hook and said, "I know you'll be busy as a paper hanger in a windstorm for a spell, Miss Charity. What say I meet you after work at our ice cream hang out across the way?"

Then he ticked his hat brim to her and lit out before she could say yes or no. Before you set the hook you let your little fish run with the bait a spell, giving it time to spit it out or swallow. He figured his chances might improve if he let her picture them walking her home for the rest of her work day. If she was interested she was interested, but trying to reel her in before there was much point to it would be dumb. He wanted her hooked and landed before he asked for a look at their books. He felt certain she'd admit to fornication with her father before she'd tattle on one of their depositers. So he had to get her to where she was willing to admit she'd fornicated with her father before he ever asked about darker secrets.

Seeing he had hours to kill and wasn't really up to any more flavored ice, Longarm got out of the sun in an establishment dispensing stronger refreshments. The saloon advertised beer on ice. Longarm asked how they managed all that ice in Wichita Falls as the barkeep laced his iced beer with Maryland rye.

The barkeep wasn't sure why someone had built a swamping ice plant over by the creek. But an older man leaning on the bar with a tall peaked ten gallon Stetson to account for the high heels he wore under a business suit said, "I can tell you. They'd been talking and talking about

53

a railroad down from the north. We've yet to see it. Don't know as we ever will. But a couple of Jew lunatics jumped the gun and built an ice plant here, expecting to sell tons of ice for the refrigerator cars in the sweet bye and bye."

Another regular, this one's suit a mite threadbare and his hat made of straw, laughed knowingly and said, "Understand them Jews sold out to local boys, trying to break even after they hauled all that ice-making gear up from Fort Worth by freight wagon, all disconnected in smaller pieces. Damned fools."

The prosperous stockman or cattle buyer shrugged and said, "Whatever. The point is that you can buy ice as cheap out our way as anywhere else, these days, and I have to say it's an improvement. Don't have to kill a chicken the day you mean to eat it, now, and lettuce keeps forever on cracked ice."

As he lowered an empty schooner to the bar Longarm pointed at it and silently signalled the barkeep. The important personage said he was much obliged and produced a business card, bragging he was a certified public accountant, which just went to prove you shouldn't judge a book by its ten gallon hat.

Longarm introduced himself with a flash of his badge and the conversation grew more comfortable. The CPA's handle was Uscott and the shabby-looking gent turned out to be a veterinarian called Wieder.

Both Texans naturally wanted to know what a federal lawman was doing in West Texas. So Longarm told them truthfully, "I'm trying to cut the trail of a hired gun. His name's Hungerford. He escaped from me over in Fort Smith and I want him back."

The vet who likely got about a mite said, "Nobody named Hungerford in these parts. Not holding land, leastways. What makes you so sure he headed this way?"

Longarm once again had no call to lie. So he explained,

"Like I said, he's a hired gun and I hear tell of a range war brewing over to the west in your panhandle."

The two Texans exchanged astounded looks. CPA Uscott said, "First I ever heard of it. Who'd fight for range where there's so *much* of it?"

The vet nodded and said, *"Water* might be worth some feuding. But as far as I know the recently established outfits over yonder all thought to survey and sew up water rights before they moved the first cow in. They've had some trouble with outlaws, of course, but nobody's been disputing range or water, yonder."

Longarm asked what kind of trouble Wieder meant. The vet sipped some suds and decided, "Petty shit. Not half so bad as when the Comanche were still raiding. Understand some laid off New Mexico hands have run off a few strays. Bad apple called Rudabaugh, Dave Rudabaugh, leads them."

The CPA said, "Some of my clients in the cattle business have said it was time the Rangers did something about that bunch."

A firm and not too friendly voice announced to the back of Longarm's neck, "Rudabaugh's bunch has recently joined forces with Jesse Evans, Doc Scurlock, Charlie Bowdrie and Billy the Kid. Or so they say, I take Doc, Charlie and the Kid in Texas with a grain of salt."

As Longarm turned to see the German silver star on an older man's vest he nodded and declared, "I was fixing to pay a courtesy call on you down the road a piece, Marshal."

The town law soberly asked, "Have your boots been stuck in dog shit? You've been in town all day, Longarm. Didn't they ever tell you it's rude to strut around another lawman's town with your nose in the air?"

The newcomer so addressed replied, "They wired you I was coming, eh? If we were alone I'd be in better shape to explain, Marshal."

The older man took him gently but firmy by one arm and led him away from the bar, sitting them both at an empty corner table as he firmly declared, "We're alone, now. What's the story?"

Longarm earnestly replied, "Opportunism. I failed to call on you this morning because I was too tired to think straight before I got set up and caught some sleep. Having nothing new to report I thought I'd drop by a certain bank and ask some delicate questions. Your Banker Gichrist turned me down."

The town law said, "Gilchrist is a banker. What more can you say against any man? What did you want to ask him?"

Longarm decided it made more sense to stay on the level, seeing he was sunk if a whole town was in cahoots with a crooked lawyer. He told his fellow lawman, "Wanted a look at the bank records of Lawyer W.R. Lovecraft. Might you know who I'm talking about?"

The town law said, "I do. I take back what I said about banker being the worse thing you can call a man. Lawyer has it beat by half. So how come you wanted the one cocksucker to show you the other cocksucker's bank records?"

Longarm said, "Small town lawyers tend to mostly small town legal chores, such as drawing up wills and contracts, getting local miscreants off on small town charges and so forth. So when you retain a small town lawyer to defend a murder case in another state you are going to pay him a sobering retainer. When and if I learn who paid such a retainer in a vain attempt to get a hired killer off, I'll have a better notion who that hired killer might still be working for."

The older lawman nodded and decided, "Makes sense to me. How come you never came by my office after Gilchrist turned you down?"

Longarm said, "I meant to. First I needed to sit down and cool off. As luck would have it, whilst I was doing so,

I got to spring for some lime sorbet and set up a walk-home after five with a gal who works at Gilchrist's bank. I came in here to stay cool as the hour hand crawls and I'll tell you what I found out as soon as I find anything out."

The older man smiled for the first time and confided, "I've heard tell of your ways with womenkind, Longarm. Is it true about you and that Treasure of France, Miss Sarah Bernhardt?"

Longarm soberly replied, "On my honor as an enlisted man it ain't. I was assigned to bodyguard the Treasure of France when she toured our west a spell back. I got to ride with her and her French theatrical troupe aboard her private train and the Divine Sarah treated me all right. She cooked and served me Crappy Susans in her underwear but that is all of her divinity I got to see and I never laid eyes on the alligator she's supposed to keep as a pet nor that coffin they say she sleeps in. As I told an infernal reporter at the end of our time together, Miss Sarah behaved more like a big sister than a boss to her help and a pure lady to yours truly."

He didn't offer to lick anyone in Texas who said this might not be so and nobody ever asked him about those other French gals aboard that train. So what the hell.

Having gotten straight with the local law, who said his pals called him Galveston, Galveston Maguire, Longarm went back to the bar to bullshit some more, nursing his suds with an eye on the clock above the back-bar and then it was time to get on back to that ice cream parlor and have a seat as he waited to see whether Charity left by the front or back door of the bank across the way.

As she served him a chocolate soda for a change the teenaged waitress told him, "She fancies you. I can tell. But girls as shy as that one are inclined to spook when you try to mount them without warning."

Longarm sternly suggested he had no such intentions.

The young sass asked, "In that case why are you waiting for her?"

57

Longarm laughed in spite of himself and told a dirty notion her words had aroused to go back where it came from. For the old saw that fifteen would get you twenty would surely apply if her parents pressed charges.

He suspected she might not address her elders with such a fresh mouth once she got old enough for the grown men she teased to take her up on it. They said Queen Elizabeth had had a filthy mouth, once more than one man had literally lost his head over her. But unlike either of them, Longarm knew he had to watch his step that evening.

So he rose to his feet and doffed his hat but kept his grin under control when Charity Barnes came out at last to head right across the street at him. He managed not to comment on how he'd about given up after all those others had left ahead of her and the hands on his pocket watch crept past five. When he asked if she felt like a soda or more sorbet she confided, "I'd rather get on home to change into something fresher, Custis. It's starting to cool off outside but you'd swear you were in one of those Indian steam baths across the way!"

So he walked her home. It wasn't far in a town that size. And from the way she helped herself to his arm he suspected she'd been picturing such a walk for some time.

Her place turned out a small frame bungalow shaded by chinaberry trees and possessed of indoor plumbing. You could tell at a glance when a new house had indoor plumbing. There was no outhouse in the back yard.

She still depended on oil lamps, though, and asked if he minded if she served supper in the dark until things cooled off some more.

As he shucked his hat and coat she added, "I'm dying! My unmentionables are soaked with . . . glow and as long as I have to change I mean to take a quick cold shower! I hope you don't think I'm being too bold!"

Longarm chuckled fondly and said, "Not hardly, Miss

Charity. I've been glowing some myself and if I knew you better I'd be tempted to ask if I might join you."

He instantly regretted what he'd just said as the mousy brunette froze in the doorway to her bath, regarding him owl-eyed in the uncertain light.

Longarm was sure he'd muffed it. She was fixing to throw the hook and swim away.

Then she softly replied, "Why don't you? I feel certain that might save us a lot of time . . . getting to know me better."

Chapter 7

Longarm was hardly the first man who'd ever noticed the brassy gal who sang bawdy songs around the piano or suggested kissing games was most likely to throw a hissy fit when a man copped a feel. Whilst the shy little librarian or in this case head stenographer was most likely to respond like a swarm of soft wet bees, trying to tongue him all over at once.

So he was in her before he finished scrubbing her back, hanging on to the shower fixtures to keep them from busting bones on the wet tiles as she tried to swallow him alive with her ring dang doo, both her legs wrapped around his waist and both of them all slathered with soap.

They wound up doing it right across her bedstead and then went back in the shower to cool off, only to wind up slathered some more.

They finally got around to dining in the dark, stark naked, along about nine. By then it had cooled enough for her to scramble them some bacon and eggs. Iced black coffee made with man-made ice from her cork-lined icebox revived him some. As they got back in bed together for dessert he was still trying to coin the proper phrasing in his mind. He knew he couldn't always count on letting slip the

61

words she'd been wanting to hear, she said, since first she'd laid eyes on him at the bank. Before he'd ever saved her life with lime sorbet.

But ponder as he might, there seemed no graceful way to ask a bank employee to sneak him into her bank for a look at the books. But in the end, the quiet little example of uncommon sense took the bit in her shy little teeth.

As they were sharing a smoke, after she'd confessed she'd never tried a "cigar" before, Charity calmly came right out and asked him why he'd really wanted to fuck her.

Longarm exploded in laughter, hastily snatching up the cheroot and brushing the tobacco sparks off the bedding they lay on before they could burn the house down around them as he asked her, "What kind of a question is that, little darling? Ain't you looked in your mirror of late?"

She calmly replied, "I have. I spend hours in front of my mirror, trying to do something about me. I know I'm not deformed. Other men have assured me I'm pretty and I suppose I almost make it. But I know what I have to offer and it's true what they say about Hell at it's most spiteful is a place called *Mediocrity*!"

"I know what you mean." said Longarm, not sure what she meant.

She sighed, "No you don't. You're a head taller than mediocre and you have the face and figure of a matinee idol. One of the tellers at the bank says you're famous as well. You're the best-looking man and the greatest lay this girl has ever had and so what are we doing in bed together if you don't want something more than . . . this?"

He set the smoke aside to pet what she referred to as her *this* and assured her it felt swell. He said. "Don't be so hard on yourself, Miss Charity. At the risk of turning your pretty little head I've been in this position with gals who couldn't hold a candle to you, and glad I was. For to tell the truth gals who resemble Miss Ellen Terry or Miss Lotta Crabtree come few and far between."

She sobbed, "Don't the rest of us know it! Have you ever read that tale about this world we're stuck in being Hell, the place we've all been sent to pay for sins in some other world?"

Longarm chuckled and replied, "Not hardly. If we're all in Hell after dying in some other world, how come we don't remember it?"

She said, "That's easy. As the author put it, we'd just give up and quit trying if we knew we were in Hell and that all our efforts would go for naught!"

Longarm conceded, "That bird had a wicked imagination. But I follow his drift and I'm sure glad it ain't so!"

She sniffed, "I'm not so certain. Don't you see how most of us just . . . never quite make it? Think how many men are forced to stand five foot eleven instead of six feet. Think what it feels like to be only a few pounds under or overweight, and unable to gain or lose those few pounds! Think of the authors who've written books that neither succeed nor fail. The violinists who play just well enough to play in an orchestra but know they will never play enough to solo! Think of us girls, so many girls, who will never quite be beautiful no matter how we try! Think of all the also-rans and tell me this isn't Hell!"

He shook his head, kissed the part of her hair, and strummed her banjo harder as he objected, "Your own comparisons prove you wrong, no offense. If *mediocre* means no more nor less than medium or average, the very term calls for most of us being mediocre. If every woman on earth woke up resembling Ellen Terry then *that* would be the average and we'd have to find something more unusual to admire in a gal. Say three tits or an eye in the middle of her forehead."

That got her to laughing.

He pursued the line of reasoning with, "Answer me this if we're all in Hell, you poor suffering sinner. How do you account for those of us as *ain't* mediocre? What are all the damsels fair and handsome devils doing in Mediocrity if that's your notion of Hell?"

She sniffed, "That's easy. You were the biggest sinners of all in our past existence. As I said, the punishment is to *almost* make it. Think what it must feel like to start out like Ellen Terry or Edwin Boothe and then get . . . *old*! Think what Alexander must have felt like after he had no further worlds to conquer as he lay there dying of the ague as a living god with the looks of an Adonis? And what about your fame as a tracker who always gets his man? Didn't it feel like Hell when Big-Chief-Walks-On-Water spit in your face this very day?"

Longarm conceded, "He didn't exactly spit in my face. It was more frustrating. I had to grin and bear it when I was itching to knock him flat!"

She snuggled closer and put her hand on his wrist to encourage what he was up to down there as she cooed, "Welcome to Hell. What did you want from the old fuss? Wait! Don't talk to me, darling! *Do* me!"

So he did her. It wasn't hard when you put it in hard. But after they'd come that way she wanted more. So he rolled her over to do her dog style, which as most couples learn a few nights into a honeymoon, or a shack job, allows for a relaxed prolonged approach to the gates of paradise in an often conversational mood.

By then it might have been too dark to see what he was doing had not the moon come up to shine in through her lace curtains and trace pretty patterns of shadow and moonlight on her bare skin as it rippled some.

He told her how great her bare ass looked by specked moonlight.

Charity replied, with a cheek on her face pressed to a pillow, he'd been about to tell her what he'd wanted from old Gilchrist.

When he told her Charity said, "It would be worth his job to let you at the books *with* a court order backing you!

64

We keep two sets of books in any case. What do you suspect him of?"

Thrusting in a rotary motion, Longarm replied, "Ain't after anybody at your bank. Wanted a look at the recent deposits of Lawyer W. R. Lovecraft is all."

She arched her spine to take it deeper as she confided, "I couldn't help you there if I wanted to, and I need my job. Mister Gilchrist keeps the records of such important depositors under lock and key. Are you talking about those unusually large retainers Lawyer Lovecraft has been depositing of late?"

He said he sure was, gripping a hip bone in either hand to underscore the earnestness of his desires, both ways.

Charity purred, "Ooh, yess! That's the way I like it. I can't give you any figures, but of course we've all been talking about the five figure checks deposited to Lovecraft and Gamble in the past quarter."

"Who's Gamble?" he asked, awaiting her answer with bated shaft.

She pleaded, "Don't tease me. Keep going. There isn't any Gamble. He just made that up to sound citified. Until he went to work for Big Dutch Steinmuller he was just a small time legal hack in a one horse town, County seat or not."

Longarm naturally wanted to know who Big Dutch Steinmuller might be.

Charity said, "I've never met him. He banks, a lot, in Fort Worth. I understand he's a cattle king, over in the panhandle. Never comes in from his swamping spread in person. They say it's a regular castle made of prairie sod. He sends flunkies, such as Lawyer Lovecraft, to do his bidding as he lords it over his Lazy S spread. That's all I really know about him. Big Dutch Steinmuller is more a presence or a puppet master plucking strings from afar. I don't thnk anyone here in Wichita Falls has ever seen him. Do you have any idea why he paid Lawyer Lovecraft all that money?"

Longarm was feeling too busy to talk at the moment. She responded in kind and they wound up half under her bed. But neither cared.

Later, helping her back in bed, Longarm told her, "Ours is not to reason why in this case. Our Big Dutch Steinmuller is recruiting an army of hard cases. The one I'm after, Frank Hungerford, never worked for Steinmuller recent. He was on the dodge from Colorado when they picked him up in the Indian Territory."

"Don't you mean Indian Nation?" she asked, adding, "Some of our depositors with Indian blood call it the Indian Nation."

He shook his head and explained, "It started out before the war as a self-governed Indian Nation. After the Cherokee in their suicidal wisom sided with the Confederacy, the winners limited their self-governing and renamed the results a territory, not a nation. Don't ever pick the losing side when you choose to go to war."

Then he blinked and said, "Hold on! You say you have depostors here in West Texas who hail from that Cherokee Rose by any other name?"

She told him they had more than one such depositor, explaining, "I understand breeds or assimilates who choose not to apply to the B.I.A. for allowances or rations are allowed to live anywhere, following any honest line of work."

He told her she was right, rolled off the bed to fumble for the note book and pencil stub in his tweeds and said, "I'm sorry, honey. I got to have some light as I take the names down."

She rose to pull down a roller shade as he fumbled out a match and lit her bedside lamp. He blinked in pleased surprise when he saw her stark by lamplight, muttering, "You call tits like that *mediocre?*"

Then he wrote down the four names she recalled as Indian or part Indian, all of them sounding as white if Smith,

66

Carter, Farmer and Brown qualified as white names. She said she thought Smith might be a Comanche breed. That added up when you considered how the half-breed Chief Quanah had been thriving in the cattle business since he'd sworn off being a wild Indian. Resettled on new range along West Cache Creek or not, with the blessing of the B.I.A., the half-white chief was charging or extorting a buck and a quarter an acre, per season, from stockmen of any complexion who admired all that grass.

But if Smith was Comanche, he failed to fit snug with a hired gun out to gun Osage near Tulsa Town and Marshal Fagan had a Kansas suspect for that confusion.

He decided to keep the names on the back of the stove for now as he studied harder on Big Dutch Steinmuller.

Now that he had some names to work with, it shouldn't be too tough to find out why Big Dutch felt he needed some serious gun hands out to his Lazy S. Nobody fights a range war or any sort of war like a shadow boxer in private. Learning who might be against Big Dutch beat riding out to the Lazy S like Froggy-Come-A-Courting to ask if they had any escaped killers he might have a word with.

It might or might not be lawful, but anyone could see a lone lawman out to arrest say Major Murphy during that Lincoln County War might have been well advised seek backup from the Tunstall McSween Faction whilst Sheriff Brady or Jim Dolan would have been the boys to buy a round for before he moved in on Tunstall or McSween.

When he trimmed the lamp Charity said, "Goody!" and jumped out of bed to let the balmy evening air back in.

Then, seeing she was on her feet for a change, she scampered into her kitchen to rustle up more iced coffee with some soda crackers. As she rejoined him Charity wistfully asked, "How early in the morning do you mean to ride on to the Lazy S, dear?"

Accepting the black coffee he was really starting to need, Longarm told her, "Nobody with a lick of sense rides blind into a buzz-saw. I can't ask anybody else to back such a play before I know what might be called for. So I got to study on Big Dutch Steinmuller and his outfit before I ride over to your panhandle."

He washed a nibble of soda cracker down and added, "To begin with, your panhandle alone is bigger than many an eastern state. Hats ain't the only things a tad oversized in Texas. So I got to find the Lazy S on the map. After that I need to know more about its owner. Any man who'd expend serious money to send first a sharp lawyer and when that didn't work a team of hired killers to the rescue of a famous professional assassin can hardly be described as a law-abiding priss. Yet nobody I've talked to out this way, so far, has said a word against him. So I've got to scout up somebody who can offer an educated guess as to what Big Dutch could be up to!"

She asked a dumb question. He sipped more iced coffee and explained, "The Tinker Kid and Artistic Algernon had to have been sent to work on the sly with Lawyer Lovecraft. It took the three of them to set up that dodge involving grease-penciled messages on white china. So counting the known killer they shot up that railroad terminal to set free, that makes at least three known killers Big Dutch has taken at least a fatherly interest in and such riders resemble bananas. They're yellow and they hang in bunches. So comes the cold gray dawn I'd best start with an appearance at my hotel to see if anybody's left any message then . . . let's see, I reckon I'll wire a progress report to my home office after a have a set-down with somebody at your local newspaper. Newspaper reporters will be the death of me yet, but they're usually ready to make a deal for your exclusive interview and I don't see how any gent given to collecting hired guns like stamps could avoid one fuss one reporter worth his salt might have heard of."

She softly said, "I don't, either. Who do mean to spend tomorrow night with, that snip at the ice cream parlor?"

"The thought never crossed my mind," Longarm lied, setting his coffee and crackers aside to take her in his arms again.

She tossed her own to the four winds to wrap both arms around him as she sobbed, "Oh, Custis, does that mean you still like me? I don't have any more secrets to offer and I know I'll never be pretty, but . . ."

He put a finger to her lips and sternly warned her, "Cut that out. We both know what you look like. You may not be Miss Ellen Terry but few men would toss you aside for eating crackers in bed."

Chapter 8

The printer's devil who led Longarm back and introduced them had described the portly gray-haired gent who presided over the city desk of *Wichita County Advertiser* as Gramps Graham. Who declared he'd heard about Longarm and invited him to a bentwood seat facing him across one corner of his cluttered desk. Before Longarm could get down to brass tacks a cub reporter in shirtsleeves joined them to ask Gramps if he wanted to run that rumor about Bat Masterson and Billy the Kid taking part in a friendly shooting match, for prize money.

Gramps looked pained but patiently explained, "During the Lincoln County War of '78, when the Kid was still free to engage in anything friendly, William Barclay Masterson was serving as Sheriff of Ford County in far off Kansas. As we speak, having lost re-election, Mister Masterson is serving as a deputy in Colorado whilst Billy the Kid is on the dodge out New Mexico way."

The cub reporter said, "I've heard rumors he's been raiding stock over in our panhandle."

Gramps said, "If he has there are no wants or warrants out on him in Texas and, in any event, if Bat Masterson met up with him anywhere he would not be talking about a

71

shooting match for prize money. Masterson would arrest the little son of a bitch for the bounty on his head!"

As the crestfallen cub reporter retreated Gramps called after him, "And for the record that younger Earp brother never ran Clay Allison out of Dodge because on the occasion mentioned Allison was miles away in New Mexico!"

Turning back to Longarm, Gramps grumbled, "Fool kids buy interviews with Deadwood Dick, a fictitious character made up for a penny dreadful printed in London Town, for Gawd's sake and keep describing Jesse James as a modern Robin Hood."

Longarm said, "I've always had my doubts about the motives of the *first* Robin Hood."

Then seeing he was satisfied Gramps Graham was an old-fashioned member of the Fourth Establishment, Longarm explained his need to know what they might have on Big Dutch Steinmuller of the Lazy S.

Leaning back expansively, Gramps pontificated, "His brand looks more like a sidewinder slithering across a cow than the letter S on its side. Home spread's up the Red River four days of hard riding. So Big Dutch seldom comes in off his range, himself."

Longarm said, "Already heard that. What sort of a rep might he have hither or yon?"

The long-time-in-Texas newspaper man said, "He's new to the panhandle. Everybody who isn't Comanche is new to the panhandle. Before he brought his hands and herd north from a smaller spread along the Brazos he had to grow up down that way as a second generation Dutchman, hence the nickname. Mess of High Dutch and Irish horned in on the rest of us back in '48 or so. Big Dutch talks natural, though, having been raised in Texas."

"Would you describe his as sweet-talking or tough-talking?" Longarm asked.

Graham replied, "I only interviewed him once, when he was in town to see about that railroad operation we're still waiting on. He was cordial enough to me. As his descriptive nick name says, he's a gent of High Dutch heritage who stands around six-foot-six in his stocking feet and walks around in high heeled Justins. But when we shook he never tried to impress me with the bone crunch hands that big men are capable of. From the way his help defers to him I'd say he's used to having his orders carried out to the letter. But he spoke to them as if they were human beings and I got the impression they were devoted to him because he was that boss every high plains drifter dreams of finding at last. Understand he pays a dollar a day minimum with a top hand drawing forty-five a month or more. They say he has a Chinese cook and High Dutch housekeeper from old country to see the grub is better than the usual biscuits and gravy whilst you can eat what the Chinaman cooks off the floors swept thrice a day by Mex gals under the eagle eye of Miss Fraw Lion. That's what the Lazy S hands call the housekeeper, Miss Fraw Lion, and I got the distinct impression they were more afraid of her than they were Big Dutch."

Longarm nodded and said, "In sum, you have described a big well-run operation managed by a firm but friendly boss. What might you be able to tell me about neighbors he might not feel as kindly toward?"

Gramps frowned thoughtfully and decided, "Can't come up with any. The range out yonder being so recently vacated by Mister Lo, there's still grass and water to spare. Biggest rival Big Dutch might be concerned about would be that new Matador Outfit, recently established south of the Prairie Dog River by another Texan called Hank Campbell with the backing of a Glasgow beef syndicate. Such expanding as they've done has been done upright and fair, buying out foolish nesters for peanuts and offering fair prices to smaller outfits."

He considered, nodded, and added, "Same goes for Captain Goodnight and Big Dutch. The three of them being about as serious about cows as they come. All three of 'em seem to be canny but honest businessmen who aim for the donut instead of the hole. So far, nobody seems to be crowding the Lazy S that much, albeit it's said others out his way held their breaths when a ragged-ass nester butchered a side of Slow Elk wearing the Lazy S brand to feed his kids."

"What happened?" Longarm asked.

The newspaper man smiled and said, "I wasn't there, but I can picture that poor nester pissing his pants when Lazy S riders brought him and the branded hide in to show Big Dutch. They say Big Dutch was sitting on the veranda of his big sod mansion, enjoying laced lager in the cool of the evening, when they tossed the incrimination hide and the nester who'd incriminated himself in the dooryard dust down the steps from where Big Dutch sat rocking. When the foreman asked where Big Dutch wanted them to hang the no-account starvling, their boss told 'em not to treat a neighbor so unkindly. He had a house servant fetch another chair and more needed beer so's he and the scared shitless nester could talk about Slow Elk."

"That does sound neighborly," Longarm conceded.

Gramps said, "Big Dutch knew what he was doing. After he calmed the poor wretch down with a cool drink and some rocking, Big Dutch told him he should have just come on over and *asked* if he needed grub for his hungry children. He pointed out it was easier on everybody if the kitchen just sent him home with a food basket. Poaching cattle was messy and could lead to misunderstandings. Then he offered the nester a loan to tide them over 'til they managed a cash crop and when the nester allowed he just couldn't see how he was ever going to reap a cash crop on marginal short-grass range Big Dutch offered him a more than fair price for his unproven claim and after the nester and his hungry family hauled out he had his hands flatten the homestead, tear out the bob wire, and restore the range to the way it had been, all without firing a shot or even making a mean face at anybody."

Longarm said, "That was the sensible way to deal with nesters. I sure wish hastier cattlemen could see you don't have to pour water on a man who's drowning. So why do you suppose such a sensible cattle king feels the need for a private army?"

Gramps shrugged and suggested, "Mebbe such feeling go with being any sort of king. Can't think of a king in this world who hasn't got an army, if only to march them up and down."

Longarm shook his head and said, "Armies are expensive toys and as the expenses mount it gets ever more tempting to put an army to work at chores that might show some damned profit."

Gramps soberly agreed, "Wars being the chore armies are best put to for fun and profit. But, as you said, armies are dangerous toys. Louis Napoleon might still be President of France had he stuck to paving highways and rebuilding Paris, France. But feeling the need to march toy soldiers up and down all those new boulevards he recruited him one hell of an army and then, having an army . . ."

"He forgot armies ought to be armed with the latest weapons," Longarm cut in, adding with a wry smile, "The Prussians had a marginally smaller army armed with those deadly needle guns and next thing Louis knew it was Prussian boots marching up and down his boulevards. It's dumb to start wars without good reason and everybody I talk to seems to think Big Dutch Steinmuller is sharp as a tack. So what am I missing?"

The newspaper man suggested, "What if there's nothing to miss? What if Big Dutch hasn't been planning any trouble at all?"

Longarm grimaced and said, "That trouble in Fort Smith was planned by Steinmuller's lawyer and paid for by retainers Steinmuller signed the checks for. Whether I've

75

beaten them here or they're still on the way, Hungerford, Rom and Jackson are guns for hire, not cooks, housekeepers nor cowhands, and who's to say how many others of their kind I might find out at the Lazy S?"

"Don't go there, then," warned Gramps, advising, "Sheriff Maguire don't have the jurisdiction in unincorporated country that far west, but the Texas Rangers do and they'd a station over on the Red River, an easy day's ride from here."

Longarm shook his head and asked, "What am I supposed to ask of any other lawman, a helping hand across the street lest I step in horse shit? You can't ask a Ranger company to saddle up and follow after you *one* day in the saddle before you swear out a complaint for them. And so far all I have on Big Dutch is suspicion. In the unlikely event any prosecuting attorney would touch what I have with a ten foot pole, Lawyer Lovecraft would only have to tell the judge and jury Big Dutch paid him all that money for other legal chores."

Gramps asked, "Didn't you say Lovecraft left more evidence over in Fort Smith, commencing with what he has going there if nobody wanted to pay for his time?"

Longarm sighed, "Still circumstantial. You can't convict on the stench of rotting fish. You have to produce the fish. It hardly seems fair, but lawyers are allowed to defend accused felons for free. They call it *pro bonum* in lawyer talk and must do it now and again for practice. They say Lovecraft is slicker than most. I aim to study him some before he notices I'm interested in his trip to Fort Smith."

Gramps said he was sorry he hadn't been more help as Longarm got to his feet. Longarm held out a hand to say, "You've been a big help, Gramps. My boss calls what we've been up to the process of eliminating and you've convinced me the Lazy S ain't run by a hot-headed bully boy. Whatever old Steinmuller is up to, it's certain to be something I ain't guessed yet!"

They shook and parted friendly. Feeling all talked out with hours to kill before he could remount Charity, Longarm went back to his hotel to change into blue denim, saddle old Buscadero, and mount him instead of Charity for a canter down the Wichita. Neither of them had pressing business down that way. But horseflesh, like the human kind, got out of shape without exercise, and poor Buscadero had been stabled for going on eighteen hours. You could tell how tedious he'd found that as they loped down the west bank, shaded by the chinaberry, box elder, cottonwood and such.

Chinaberry trees didn't hail from China any more than box elders came in boxes. They'd always grown in West Texas to hear Reservation Comanche piss and moan about how they missed their inedible chinaberries.

They were called that because they looked to be fashioned from white chinaware. Some said they were poison. Others said they wouldn't hurt you but tasted like bird shit. Longarm had never asked how anyone might know what birdshit might taste like and just didn't bother with eating chinaberries.

After that they grew on brushy trees that cast more shade than the taller cottonwood or ragged-ass box elders. The Wichita of West Texas had nothing to do with the Wichita Indians of Kansas, who once you got them to confess, allowed Wichita was just another half-ass attempt at *wichasha*, meaning any human being in their dialect. That notorious Washita where Custer had shot those ponies was another try at the same meaning. They called white folk *Wasichu* and spelled that more than one way. Reporters and barroom bullshit artists were forvever trying to shoehorn western legend involving the two Red Rivers, the two Virginia Cities and multiple Bent's Forts into coherent if impossible yarns and it seemed as easy to turn a cattle king with a private army into a Santa Claus of the plains as it was to buy Miss Calamity Jane Cannary's claim she'd graciously granted James Butler Hickok a divorce in Deadwood, as they were building it, so's he could marry Miss Agnes Lake. As he had managed, in fact, before coming out to a spanking new gold camp for the first time. To apply for a job as Town Law.

"A cattle king recruiting a private army is a cattle king getting set to give somebody a hard time!" Longarm assured his mount as they headed back from their constitutional.

He'd just reined in to walk his mount the rest of the way back to the hotel stable when he was hailed by a bucktoothed kid with a pewter star pinned to his sweat shirt.

Longarm wheeled Buscadero over to him to see what he wanted. The young deputy said, "I just come from your hotel. I been looking all over for you. You sure are a hard man to find!"

Longarm replied, "You found me. What's up?"

The kid said, "Sheriff Maguire sent me to find you. He figured you ought to know!"

Longarm snorted, "I never thought the tooth fairy sent you. What in thunder ought this child to know?"

The squirt said, "Sheriff says to tell you Big Dutch Steinmuller just rode into town with a dozen Lazy S riders. They're over to the Sam Houston Saloon and the sheriff says Big Dutch seems upset about something. He thought it might be better if you heard about it first from us. Sheriff says we can hide you out over to our office if you'd like."

Longarm said, "Tell him I'm much obliged, but I've always felt that when you get a boil on your ass it's best to lance the son of a bitch and get it over with."

Chapter 9

Once he'd seen to his horse and saddle Longarm and his yellowboy were moving down the shady side of the street towards the Sam Houston Saloon, as one called the place he'd been drinkig the day before in less ominous company. A city block short, Sheriff Maguire and a younger man who looked like an Anglo just back from Old Mexico in his silver-trimmed black charro duds and slate gray sombrero fell in to either side of him. The sheriff introduced the stranger as Rube Shire from Singer's Wells and added, "Close as anything resembling a town to the Lazy S. Rube says he's on good terms with Big Dutch."

Rube Shire, handsome as well as Anglo under that big Mex hat, once you peered deep in its shade, asked, "What's this all about, Longarm? Is it all right to call you Longarm? I've read about you in the *Police Gazette*."

Longarm said, "You can call me anything but late for breakfast but I wish the *Illustrated Police Gazette* would stick to whoppers about two-headed calves and magic cures for baldness. I am headed for the Sam Houston Saloon because I understand it's infested with Lazy S riders. Sheriff Maquire, here, can tell you what I want with the same."

"Toting a Winchester?" marveled Rube Shire, "Big Dutch Steinmuller and his hands are good old boys. They never rode in for a shoot-out with anybody!"

"Then why did they ride in?" asked Longarm.

The man who claimed to know them better replied, "I don't know. I just heard they were in town."

Maguire said, "I sent for Rube when I heard *he* was in town as well. He just moved out yonder from here in Wichita Falls. So I figured a gent with a foot on both bases might help us grease the goings. I'd as soon not have a total disaster betwixt the federal government and an outfit as big as the Lazy S on my hands!"

Rube Shire suggested, "Let me tote that Winchester, Longarm. It'll look more natural in my hands, seeing I just rode in across Indian country."

Longarm said, "Get your own yellowboy. I paid for this one. Where did you get that *rurale* hat?"

The almost as tall Texan easily replied, "Off a *rurale*. I was minding my own business in Ciudad Acuna when this *rurale* in his cups called me a *gringo chingado* and asked if I wanted to dance. The rest you can guess. I've heard about *El Brazo Largo* and *Los Rurales*. What do you reckon makes them so mean?"

Sheriff Maguire opined, *"Chili* peppers. Nobody can grow up natural on *chili con carne* and hot *tamales*. After that they don't allow you to be a Mexican lawman if you can read and write."

Rube Shire warned, "Steinmuller and his Lazy S riders don't act like mean drunks. But don't take them for sissies, neither. Treat Big Dutch right and he'll meet you halfway."

"What happens if you cross him?" Longarm asked, with sincere interest.

The man who claimed to know him better said, "He's never had no trouble up this way. Some years ago, down along the Brazo, they say he killed a man. Bare-handed. After the cuss shot him. Then he payed for the drunk's funeral and sent his effects home to Tennessee with a letter of condolence. After that nobody ever mess with Big Dutch when he came to town."

Longarm whistled and asked, "Where was he shot?"

Rube Shire said, "Through the right lung, or so I hear. Big man with a big chest can take a .44-40 round through mostly empty space and still wring your neck like a chicken's. Wound never mortified. So he went on about his business as if nothing had happened."

"His business being . . . ?" asked Longarm.

Shire said, "Cows. Big Dutch grew up knowing all there was to know about cows. His elders had raised cows in their old country. Big Dutch rode with Hood's Brigade in the war and after that failed to finish him, he got in on the postwar beef killings, where you could buy Texas beef at four dollars a head, drive 'em north to the cross country rail lines and unload 'em for twenty. As we speak he's increasing his herd natural or paying ten dollars a head for calves he can fatten to forty dollar cows on buffalo grass the buffalo ain't using any more."

Longarm nodded and said, "In sum we are talking about a mighty rich bird it takes more than a .44-40 to stop."

"But neighborly," Rube Shire insisted.

Longarm said they'd see about that as he led the way across a short expanse of sun-baked street dust towards the batwing doors of the Sam Houston Saloon. They heard the buzz of conversation until they got inside.

Then it got so quiet you could have heard a flea fart. There was no mystery as to which of the trail-dusted riders who'd taken the place over had to be Big Dutch. He was taller seated at a corner table than some managed standing up. He seemed to be holding court behind a scuttle of draft, dressed for riding but more expensively in a black silk shirt under snow white ten-gallon-and-top-of-the-line Stetson. His face looked as if it had been carved from a well-cured ham, with the whittle marks barely smoothed over. His eyes were twilight blue as they stared into Longarm's with the expression of a butcher shop cat regarding a mouse hole after hours.

Rube Shire broke the ice by leading the way and introducing Longarm to His Majesty of Cows.

Big Dutch said, "Set down, the three of you, and we'll fix you all up with beer steins. I'm glad you dropped by, Longarm. Saves us the time and trouble of scouting you up."

As Longarm and the two on his side settled into captain's chairs that appeared out of nowhere, Steinmuller said, "Understand you were looking for Lawyer Lovecraft when you first arrived. That makes two of us. He was supposed to drive out to my spread. He never did. I've been wondering why. What did you want with him, pard?"

Longarm waited as a cuss who looked important enough to be a segundo or at least a top hand produced three steins from the bar and poured from the scuttle on the table. Longarm noticed Big Dutch thanked him by the name of Mister Horn.

Mister Horn murmured, "*Por nada, Patron*," and evaporated.

Longarm figured there were at least a dozen guns covering him as he replied with the yellowboy across his thighs under the table, "I had a prisoner escape from me in Fort Smith. I want him back. I was given to understand Lawyer Lovecraft from these parts defended the killer in court. Wanted to ask him if he had any suggestions."

Big Dutch said, "Banker Gilchrist tells me you were after him about who might have paid for the defense of young Frank Hungerford. He said he never told you. So who told you?"

Longarm sipped some suds and asked, "Who says anybody told me?"

Big Dutch said, "When a man stops asking questions he knows the answers. Would you care to hear why I sent my lawyer to defend the boys?"

Longarm allowed he sure would.

Steinmuller said, "Ain't laid eyes on young Frank Hungerford since he was a kid. Understand he grew up sort of wild. But I knew his folk down on the Brazos, years ago, and it ain't as if I can't afford to lend a hand for old time's sake. So I paid Lawyer Lovecraft, handsome, to see if he could get the boy off. As you know, he couldn't. You have my word as a man I know nothing about that shoot-out in the railroad terminal. I never heard of those other gunslicks. Frank must have sent for them on his own."

Longarm figured accusing a cattle king's lawyer whilst surrounded by a cattle king's crew could take fifty years off a man's life. So he asked if Tinker Kid or Artistic Algernon meant anything to any of them. Steinmuller said, "Never on my payroll. Mister Horn?"

The lean and hungry-looking rider so addressed said, "Never heard of a Tinker Kid. Algernon Jackson is a horse thief of color they describe as artistic because of his skills with a running iron. He's said to have run brands for both sides during that Lincoln County War. He's a pure professional who feels no loyalty to our kind."

Steinmuller gravely thanked him and turned back to Longarm to explain, "Mister Horn is a range detective who would know about such things. I've hired him away from The Pinkertons to avoid misunderstandings as we all settle in on new range. The bigger outfits know better than to slap a brand on a calf in the company of another man's cow, but some newcomers to the industry will take chances."

"What do you do to them when they cut a Lazy S calf out of the consolidated herd at roundup time?" asked Longarm.

Steinmuller easily replied, 'That's why I keep Lawyer Lovecraft on a handsome retainer. When you hang a cow thief from a cottonwood tree his kith and kin are inclined to remember. When a kissing cousin spends some time making little rocks out of big ones you don't want to talk about him. Ain't had to put anybody in jail since we resettled up this way. Had way more troubles down along the Brazos. That was one of the reasons we resettled up this way."

Longarm sipped more suds and allowed he'd heard about Big Dutch and that hungry nester.

The cattle king smiled modestly and replied, "Oh, that? Didn't need a college degree to see a widow and four hungry orphans bawling just over your horizon added up to more trouble than a head of Slow Elk could ever be sold for. Ain't it a bitch how gossip can inflate a minor fuss with a trash neighbor into a Trojan War? I sometimes wonder if the real Trojan War amounted to more than a family feud over wife stealing. Can you see anybody launching a thousand ships, or a thousand riders, in pursuit of a runaway wife?"

Longarm laughed at the picture and replied, "Folk do tend to inflate the numbers when describing things out our way."

He knew better than to ask exactly how much Big Dutch had paid Lawyer Lovecraft, whether he'd known about those extra expenses involving grease pencils and hired guns or not. He was trying to figure a way to get himself invited out to the Lazy S without a search warrant when Big Dutch said, "When and if you catch up with my lawyer, tell the elusive cuss I said he was to lay the cards out on the table for you. I ain't got time to search further for him. We was only passing through on our way to Fort Worth, where I've more serious rows to hoe."

Sheriff Maguire, Lord love him, asked how come Big Dutch had rows to hoe in Fort Worth.

Big Dutch didn't sound at all evasive as he answered, easily, "When a mountain won't come to your momma's kin you got to go ask the mountain why you can't have a railroad like the other kids. We've been waiting and waiting for them to run us some rails down from the north or up from the south. We got all that beef out on the range waiting to be shipped on the hoof or slaughtered and sent refrigerated. But we're still driving the poor brutes north the way we were driving them back in the sixties!"

He nodded at Shire and said, "You know what I'm talking about, Rube. Would you rather go on selling ice to housewives, butchers and such or sell it by the tons a car to mile long eastbound trains?"

Rube Shire sighed and said, "I wish you hadn't said that, Dutch. Makes me think of this long ago gal who extorted flowers, books and candy for no more than kisses on a porch swing with her little brother playing on the steps!"

He explained to Longarm, "I have more irons in the fire here in this future rail center than the town has fire. Breaking even on my ice plant, coal yard, empty stockyards I built and such. That's how come I know these Lazy S riders so well, of late. Been moving some of my attempts to get rich out their way. Starting with a lumber yard in Singer's Wells. At the rate I'm going I may have to seek public office as the last resort of the luckless."

Sheriff Maguire said, "Thanks a heap, you damnyankee!"

He went on to explain to Longarm, "Old Rube's a carpetbagger gone native. Rode for the Reconstruction's State Police 'til Washington came to its senses and reconstructed our Rangers. Tell him how you got started as a venture capitalist with that bounty money, Rube."

Shire looked down at his suds and muttered, "Texas *wanted* the sons of bitches, didn't it?"

It was Big Dutch who chuckled fondly and said, "Rube's a wonder at tracking Mex border raiders, even when they make her back to Mexico. He don't just dress Mexican. He talks Mexican and *thinks* Mexican on the trail of a Mexican outlaw. Made hisself a real bundle a few years back, rounding up a whole gang with bounties on every head."

Rube Shire said, "Aw, cut it out. I'm in the coal, ice and lumber trade now. With loading pens to let if they ever build that infernal railroad."

Big Dutch expansivley replied, "I'll put in a word for your loading yard in Fort Worth when we get there."

He drained his own stein and added, "Ain't about to get there drinking beer on our rumps!"

He rose to his full height, higher than Longarm was expecting, and bellowed, *"Vamanos, muchachos!* Last one in to Fort Worth is a girl!"

As his crew stomped out ahead of him Big Dutch casually asked Rube Shire when he meant to head back to Singer's Wells. Shire replied he meant to spend the night in town and Longarm was pleased as punch.

He'd been wondering how he was going to tag along with a rider who'd be accepted in a dinky trail town, in a manner Big Dutch might not be aware of.

For the courts and pests like Lawyer Lovecraft could be so picky about search warrants or the lack thereof but, what the hell, a well-meaning lawman riding all the way out yonder at the invite of a local businessman could hardly be expected to need a search warrant if he wanted to pay a call on another pal as long as he was out that way. Could he?

Charity Barnes agreed it sounded innocent enough to her as they had supper together in the nude.

When she asked how he meant to wrangle an invite to such a long ride from Rube Shire Longarm allowed he had all night to work on that. So she clapped her hands and said, "Goody! Let's go to bed and put our heads together!"

Chapter 10

They woke up before dawn confounded and sneezing with their eyes full of grit. Charity was screaming, "The window! Shut the window!" as Longarm staggered about blindly to accomplish this with the wind blowing like hell inside her bungalow.

By the time they'd showered together and rinsed the grit out of their eyes they agreed on what had just happened. Such dry dusters blew out of the desert lands to the southwest rarely, but when they blew they sure left a mess to clean up.

Longarm suggested they let the fine wind-blown dust settle a spell before they tried to sweep it out with the wind still howling hard enough to shake the frame bungalow and rattle the shut doors and windows. Charity hauled all the dusty bedding off the mattress and replaced it with fresh crisp cotton from her linen closet so they could get back in bed to ride the duster out. That was what Charity called it when she got on top, riding a duster out.

The duster was still gusting on and off as they had breakfast in bed, with her scrambled eggs a little gritty. But by nine it had blown over and the cheerful birds were twittering in the chinaberry trees out back as if they were celebrating the end of a rain storm. You had to think flexible to be a bird in West Texas.

Longarm filled a bottle with tap water and using his thumb as a sort of loose stopper, sprinkled the dust carpet all over the floors to lay it some before he dared to herd most of it out the front or back door with a push broom. Charity worked as naked in his wake with a damp dust cloth, smugly telling him how lucky he'd been every quarter hour or less. He'd known before she'd bragged on it he and old Buscadero would have been in a hell of a mess if an early departure had put them out on the trail when that duster tore in without warning. He'd have spoiled her day had he told her he hardly ever rode out across the range before cockscrow, even when he didn't have anybody to scout up before he left. So he never.

He knew Rube Shire would hardly have left town with that duster in full force and he'd likely take his time getting set to ride anywhere, now. So Longarm was a sport about helping Charity tidy up before he took another shower with her, tore off a morning quickie, and needed another shower before he got dressed to go looking for that accidental meeting with old Rube whilst Charity went off to her job at the bank.

He tried first at the coal yard, where Rube supplied coal hauled in from the railhead by wagonloads to the kitchen ranges, hot water heaters and steam boilers of Wichita Falls.

He had competition, of course, but Longarm didn't expect to find Rube Shire working for any of his rivals.

Nobody at his coal yard had seen him that morning, either. Longarm thanked them and tried the ice house. The clerk out front said the boss had passed through the day before, but they hadn't seen him since. When Longarm asked if he'd try, the clerk called into the back and an ice wrangler came out in an oilcloth apron with a wicked-looking set of ice tongs and a quizzical expression. He told them the boss hadn't been around to the back that morning and added they were loading the damned wagons to deliver some damned ice.

Longarm asked if they delivered ice as early as others delivered the morning milk.

The ice man shook his head and said, "Customers want ice delivered after they've fed the man of the house, sent him on his way, and put some clothes on. Don't believe all those dirty jokes about housewives and icemen. Unlike milkmen, we got to traipse through the kitchen with our ice and they don't want us to catch 'em off guard. So we usually start almost late as this, even when New Mexico ain't powdering our noses."

The clerk who took orders out front said, "There you go. Nobody was here any earlier than us so the boss must not be coming in."

Longarm said, "He told me he was riding out to Singer's Wells this morning."

The clerk shrugged and said, "Then he's rode or he ain't started yet. Have you tried at his town house?"

Longarm said, "Not hardly. I didn't know he had a house here in The Falls."

The clerk handed him a business card with the local residential address already printed on it. Longarm put it away, feeling foolish because he hadn't thought to ask about that earlier.

The cottage Rube Shrine had hung on to in Wichita Falls was only a walk from the other ventures he'd started in The Falls and Longarm found the ambitious venture capitalist in his kitchen, having the ham and eggs he'd cooked and served himself, he told Longarm, explaining the housekeeper he started out with was out in Singer's Wells. He added, "Even using this place less than a few times a month I save on hotel bills by hanging on to her."

Longarm asked if he had somebody watching it for him when he was off to the west. Rube Shire smiled wolfishly and replied, "I don't get robbed much. Don't keep anything here worth the risk to anybody with a lick of sense."

Longarm thought about the risk of robbing a known bounty hunter who wore a brace of Colt Lightnings in those shoulder holsters under his bolero. The gun slinger who'd popularized shoulder holsters not that long ago, John Wesley Hardin, was said to have killed a couple of dozen unfortunates who'd annoyed him before the Rangers put him away in Huntsville.

Fishing for an invitation, Longarm said he was glad Shire was still in town because he'd been thinking of scouting out that way and wasn't sure where Singer's Wells might be.

Rube Shire said, "You follow the Red River along its south bank most of the way. You see signs when you're getting warm. Takes most of us three days in the saddle. More than one trail flop along the way to choose from. I'd be proud to show you the way. But I ain't going back for a spell. Got a buyer interested in my ice plant. Hope springs eternal like they say."

Longarm asked, "Ain't you showing a profit from that ice plant? It seems to me they use a lot of ice in this town."

Rube Shire grimaced and replied, "Costs almost as much to make it as I can sell it for, delivering a few cakes at a time by employees who keep asking for higher wages."

He speared some ham with his fork and said, "I wasn't whistling Dixie when I told Maguire I was thinking of running for Sheriff out yonder. We don't have an incorporated county yet. But they're talking about appealing to Austin and a steady county income, backing the lumber yard and such out yonder, would allow me to sell out here in The Falls and save myself from having to juggle barely-break-even notions."

He washed the morsel down with coffee and darkly predicted, "Ain't never going to be nothing but a one horse town here. Starting over out in cow country with cow country beeswax and a county job seems the way to go. I bit off more than I can chew in this county seat. Don't let this get out, but Texans are more clannish than Scotch Highlanders and Sicilians combined. No future for a lawman who once rode for the Reconstruction here in the county seat. I figure to do better out on the panhandle range where most everyone is new."

Longarm had no idea what you might ask for a coal yard or ice plant so he could only wish the ambitious cuss luck as he left to work things out for himself. He'd already learned the banks of the Red River were fair settled as far west as he'd care to follow her across the panhandle and a slow but sure poking along was the best way to get the lay of any strange land.

He'd left his bedroll with his regular saddle and saddle gun back in Denver, never having expected the chore of transporting a prisoner to turn out so rancid. So he decided to forgo any thought of camping along the trail. Rube Shire had told him there were plenty of places to flop more comfortable along the way. So he rode out alone on Buscadero without the extra pony he might have led behind them to pack a lighter load of trail supplies and allow him to swap mounts from time to time.

Buscadero wanted to lope some more down the Wichita but Longarm held him to a trot, warning, "You won't want to travel this fast by the end of this day, old frisky."

They were headed down the Wichita to join up with the Red River before following it upstream to the west. This close to the county seat it would have been awkward to cut cross-country, what with all the bob wire fencing around the truck or dairy farms you saw within an easy wagon haul from a town of any size. The scenery that had seemed so pretty the afternoon before looked dreary and discouraging that morning.

The trees along the Wichita rose ghostly and brownish

gray against the blue sky beyond, with each dusted leaf re-sembling the wings of a night flying moth. The stream ran fresh in a startling manner betwixt banks lined with dusty sedge and cattails. The trail ahead was dusty as the floors of Charity's bungalow had been before they'd swept and mopped it that morning so's she could be late for work along with everybody else in town. He could see at a glance how few had ridden north ahead of him that late morning. Their few hoofmarks were easy to read as hoof-marks in a light snow and the occasional horse apple in the dust shone almost golden in contrast. Horseshit was a pretty shade of light brown when you studied it without prejudice.

The barley fields and meadows off the trail to either side were as dusted over. It was hard to tell meadow grass from half grown barley when it got that dusty. You drilled in bar-ley instead of corn on the high plains if you knew what you were doing. Corn was a profitable but thirsty crop you had to water like a kitchen garden out west of say Longitude 100°. Mexicans grew corn everywhere, by hand, because they hardy ate anything else, save for beans. Folk serious enough to raise crops by the acre found barley or, better yet, beef, more profitable in a land of little rain.

Longarm knew that until they got some rain, or at least a good clean breeze from some other direction, the local landscape was likely to look as dreary. Old timers said the dry winds out of the south-west hadn't been as dusty within living memory. The once grassy vales of the Pecos and Rio Grande over yonder had been overgrazed beyond common sense.

There was talk in Congress about controlling the herds allowed to graze the open range—currently open to all who cared to graze private property. But so far the politicians who drank with the beef lobby was content with talk.

A mile outside of town, just as his mount had calmed down to a slow but steady walk, Longarm met up with a wary looking yellow dog and a pair of tired-looking kids. A boy of about nine and a tag along kid sis of say seven. The boy called out, "Is it far to town, mister? Are we almost there yet?"

Longarm reined in to reply, "Not hardly, sport. I'd say you had over three miles or an hour's walk ahead of you. What's your big hurry?"

The boy said, "Momma sent us to tell the law about the man asleep in the wagon. Our pa is down the Red at a barn raising and we don't know when he'll be back so . . ."

"You say there's a man asleep in a wagon?" Longarm cut in, not having to guess why a caring mother might put things that way if she felt the need of the law.

So he flashed his badge at the kids to show he wasn't greening them as he said, "I'm the law. How far back might this wagon be?"

The boy allowed they'd been on the road at least a quarter hour or mayhaps half a mile. Longarm suggested they'd make better time if Little Sis rode Buscadero with him and she was delighted to ride sidesaddle on the skirts behind him, hugging his waist and declaring she meant to marry him when she grew up.

With the boy jogging in the lead they were soon within sight of a woman in a mother hubbard and sunbonnet, standing by the side of the trail and pointing at a gap in her bob wire. A delivery van painted mustard-colored by dust stood out in a field of dusted-over barley. The trail of flattened profit leading out to it had been dusted over as well. Someone had cut the fence and run that dray off the trail in the dark of night before that dust storm. Anything hauling it had been led back along the same path.

As Longarm reined in near their unsettled mother to swing Little Sis to the ground and allow he was a lawman at her service, she sort of sobbed, "You'd best have a look, alone, whilst I hold the children here, sir."

Longarm dismounted and tethered Buscadero to a fence

post. You never rode a horse any closer unless you knew it was cavalry-trained. The remount service got horseflesh used to gunshot and the smell of death with shots fired in the air and rotten meat upwind before it sent the same out in the field.

But as he followed the dusty swathe through the dusty but still living barley Longarm didn't smell anything bad and when he got there, just as the kid had said, the gent on his side in the back looked as if he'd crawled in to take a nap.

He was dead, of course. And stiff besides when Longarm shook his shoulder. So Longarm told him, "You've been dead about twelve hours and that works out about right. So who the hell were you?"

The bearded but well-groomed cadaver was wearing an expensive sissy suit of summerweight broadcloth. His hat, in a corner of the wagon bed he lay on, was a pearl gray Stetson with a narrower brim than Texas cow hands fancied and his boots, like Longarm's, were low-heeled for walking as much as riding.

Climbing in to get a better grasp on the subject, Longarm rolled the stiffened cuss off his side enough to get at the billfold in an inside pocket of his frock coat.

He let the cadaver lay back in position as he held the billfold in both hands, muttering, "You'll start to soften up, and then some, any time, now. In the meantime, let's see who you might have been before *rigor mortis* sets in."

It wasn't hard. The unfortunate cuss had been packing all sorts of personal identification, including business cards.

So Longarm nodded down at the remains to mutter, 'Well, howdy, Lawyer Lovecraft. I've been looking all over for you!"

Chapter 11

There went a day on the trail because Longarm naturally had to ride back to The Falls and report the murder to Sheriff Maguire. They both agreed it looked like murder before Doc Ballard, their coroner-cum-druggist, found the bullet hole in his back. A small caliber round didn't leave a dramatic entrance in black wool. Doc agreed Lovecraft had been shot around twelve hours before Longarm had caught up with him, or say ten or eleven the night before.

Their conversation was taking place back in town, a few hours later, with Lovecraft still stiff on his side but naked on the zinc-topped dissecting table under Doc's drugstore as the balding forensic expert poked the cadaver to say, "Starting to relax some. Over the next forty-eight hours he'll go mushy as a wet dishrag."

The sheriff opined, "He was murdered and hauled off into that barley field by a person or persons unknown betwixt going on midnight and that duster as blew in before dawn. But where did they shoot him? He ain't been at his office nor at his townhouse for some time. Others working for him, both places, would have noticed."

Longarm said, "I mean to send a wire to Fort Smith about the delivery dray I found him in. By now they may have more on a dray just like it, last seen fleeing the scene of a crime in a damper storm."

Maguire was quick-witted. He said, "You're suggesting them three outlaws you want finally made her here in such a dray. But why would they gun the very lawyer who helped Hungerford escape?"

Longarm said, "I mean to ask when I catch up with 'em. But as an educated guess, a slippery lawyer who met them here and led them to some hideout might have turned from an asset to a risk they wanted to eliminate."

Maguire nodded and said, "He might have told them you'd come by and he was ducking you. So they got rid of him and that incriminating transportation purloined in Fort Smith at the same time. Meaning the murdersome trio must be holed up right here in The Falls!"

Longarm warned, "Don't take the bit in your teeth and just run with the wind, Sheriff. It works as well or better another way. We know they haven't been holed up around Lovecraft's home or office. He could have been hiding from me alone and met them anywhere in town as planned back in Fort Smith. They could have loaded him in with them and driven out a ways to get rid of him and that dray before they just rode on most anywhere, say with his money and fresh mounts he had waiting for them. They'd have had no call to scout him up if he hadn't offered them a good reason."

Maguire asked, "Are you saying Lovecraft was acting as a sort of relay station for riders bound for other parts?"

Longarm said, "Three strangers, one of them colored, would be dumb to loiter about this one horse town, no offense, and Lovecraft was only in the pay of somebody richer."

Maguire whistled and pointed out, "But Big Dutch Steinmuller just rode off to Fort Worth, clean out of the county."

Longarm smiled thinly and said, "I noticed. He may

have wanted us to notice. First things coming first, we'd best begin by making sure the three of 'em ain't in town. I'll be surprised as hell if they are, but the process of eliminating calls for eliminating such shit."

As he headed for the cellar steps with the sheriff in tow, Maguire asked, "Don't you reckon I ought to posse up? They've already got a good fourteen or fifteen hours' lead on us if they're making for the Lazy S!"

Longarm said, "All the better to see you with, my dear. Rube Shire tells me the river trail is fair settled and I don't see how two white boys and a colored rider could cover all that distance without anybody noticing, do you?"

Maguire smiled sheepishly and confessed, "Not now. I see why they say you're good, Longarm. There's much to be said for this eliminating shit. Where'd you learn it?"

As they crossed the yard to the alley Longarm explained, "I work for a wise old owl who broke in with your own Rangers, under Captain Big Foot Wallace, who, I understand, could show the Comanche a thing or two about tracking. Old Billy Vail's a caution for locating hideouts miles away without getting up from his desk. First thing he pounded into me, eight or ten years ago when I gave up on herding cows, was that hunting crooks took more brainwork than hunting strays. Stray cows most often wind up where you'd expect, where there's cover, brouse and water. Crooks are forever trying to confound us. But sometimes that can give us an edge."

As they followed the alley out to the street the older but not half as experienced lawman asked, "How do you figure that? Seems crooks out to slicker us have the deck stacked in their favor."

Longarm said, "Let's hope those three feel that way. Since old Billy taught me to take time to study patterns I've learned other tracking tricks from Indian scouts I've rid with. Writers who go on about Noble Savages closer to nature than the rest of us think Indians track by some sixth sense, or like dogs sniffing the spoor of a fleeing felon."

"Don't they?" asked Maguire.

Longarm said, "Not hardly. Lacking the nose of a bloodhound but possessed of more brains, they try to think ahead of the game, enemy or whatever they're tracking. For example, when you follow hoof marks to a desert playa and you know where the next water hole is, you don't have to follow a dotted line across all that dry mud. You can short cut for that water hole and sometimes get there first to lay for the cuss if he's taking time trying to leave you a tangled trail. I once had time to enjoy a good night's sleep in a trail town hotel I'd guessed right on before my want checked in the next morning."

Maguire spied Rube Shire across the way and hailed him, calling out, "We're fixing to dragnet! Care to join in, Rube?"

The former bounty hunter with political ambitions allowed he sure would if they'd tell him what they were out to net.

They filled him in on the killing as the three of them went on to the sheriff's office, picking up a deputy making his rounds along the way.

Once he knew what they were up to the venture capitalist who owned so much of the business district of a one horse town opined, "Has to be a private home. Other than the one Lawyer Lovecraft admitted to, that is. Everyone in The Falls knew him at a distance in them high-priced duds and sissy hat he favored. Somebody would have spotted him pussyfooting around the center of things the past few days."

Longarm asked, "How come? Nobody knew he was missing before I got here to ask his whereabouts. His employees weren't acting worried and who feels it noteworthy to see a familiar figure where they're used to seeing the same?"

Shire shrugged and decided, "He'd still have to have brass balls or some place to lay low, in the business district or out on the outskirts of town if he was waiting on a secret meeting."

"Why did it have to be a secret meeting?" asked Maguire and when they both looked at him the same way he added, "Oh."

At his office, Maguire mustered four more deputies, asking Longarm if a corporal's squad, spread out, added up to enough of a dragnet.

.When Longarm allowed they might just manage, if that was all they had to work with, Rube Shire brightened and said, "I should have drunk more coffee this morning! I got another half dozen delivery men on my payroll and, better yet, they deliver coal or ice all over town! Might we not eliminate a heap of housewives they deliver to regular?"

Longarm said, "Not hardly. A mistress kept on the side by a sneaky lawyer might well require coal and ice. But we can use the extra help and, better yet, such gossip as delivery men pick up on their rounds."

So Shire delegated two deputies to run north to his separate coal and ice outfits without asking Maguire's permission. But the sheriff didn't seem to notice.

Sheriff Maguire had a heap to learn about politics if Rube Shire was sprouting political ambitions.

In any event, by mid-afternoon it was generally agreed no strangers of any description were holed up in town, unless they were in something deeper than a root cellar or more private than a locked up warehouse.

Rube Shire had his men search his ice plant, grain elevator and coal tipple in the unlikely event Lawyer Lovecraft had suggested either. They found a burnt down cigar butt nobody working the grain elevator could remember smoking, but as in the case of dirty black coal or ass-freezing ice, it hardly seemed anyone would hole up long in dusty bulk barley.

By the time they'd agreed the killer had to be long gone Longarm felt as if he'd been rolling in coal dust, shattered grain and ice plant water that had warmed up a lot since he'd made the mistake of sitting down in Shire's cavernous storage space. In a world where science kept outracing natural ways, Longarm hadn't had as much experience as Rube Shire with frozen water in high summer.

The seat of his jeans was almost dry by the time Longarm found himself alone again near Charity's bank. So he took a seat under the awning across the way to study some more about ice in summer time.

That same teenaged know-it-all took his order for iced black coffee gracefully enough. But as she placed it on the marble table in front of him, she confided in her know-it-all way, "You're wasting your time on that banking woman across the way. As I told you, yesterday, she likes you, but she's a dried up old maid who works in a *bank!*"

"That sure sounds discouraging," Longarm dryly replied before sipping some coffee.

The waitress said, "I can tell you how it went last evening when you walked her home. She led you on with encouraging words and then parted with a warm smile and a handshake on her doorstep, right?"

Longarm said, "Close as I care to go into it, Miss . . . ?"

"They call me Cup Cakes," she modestly replied.

He didn't have to ask why. June was busting out all over and it hardly seemed fair.

Like other healthy men his own age, Longarm felt the usual lusts for forbidden fruit and that included jailbait. But at the same time, like a lot of men, he admired brains in a woman almost as much or more than he lusted for firm tits and tight asses. For once you'd had your way with any sort of flesh you were stuck with the pillow talk that came after and could make a man feel disgusted with himself to find himself in bed with a dumb kid.

His perfect lover, he'd long since decided, would be an

impossible combination of youth and experience. A mature college professor gal with the face and body of a sixteen-year-old. For some of his fondest memories were of smart old gals who'd not only screwed him black and blue but *taught* him things he'd never known before as they lay there getting their second winds.

Some philosopher had once written, no doubt in French, that a man is never more sane than he feels after a good meal and a warm lay. So little known bits of Indian lore, stage magic, chemistry or even undertaking seemed to sink in better than if you'd read them in a book when they were whispered in your ear by a naked lady playing with your old organ grinder. So Longarm was more willing to forgive sagging tits than dim wits.

Miss Cup Cakes seemed to think he'd find it interesting to learn they were holding a cake sale at her church that weekend. She confided that the swain who bid the most on a cake she'd baked would get to walk her home along the shady way along the Wichita in the moonlight, past this shady bower of chinaberry trees she knew of.

When he just went on sipping iced coffee Cup Cakes confided, "I'm not supposed to tell, but the cake I baked for the sale is frosted with zebra stripes of chocolate and vanilla!"

Longarm assured Cup Cakes her secret was safe with him and she went back to the kitchen, smiling like the cat who ate the canary. Longarm sometimes felt wistful about a golden long ago when he'd felt so sure he knew all he needed to know and twice as much as his elders. But at a place called Shiloh he'd learned how much he still had to study on and he hoped Miss Cup Cakes would make it to older and not half so sure of herself without getting killed, either.

Then he saw Charity coming out of the bank across the way and rose to meet her, leaving less change but still a respectable amount for Cup Cakes on the table.

He wasn't sure he'd made the right move when he saw the look of surprised adoration on Charity's face as they met in the middle of the street.

She gasped, "Oh, Custis, darling! You've come back to me! I've been thinking of you all day and I can't wait to take you home for . . . supper."

It had been his intention to explain why he'd left town so late, in case she'd heard he was still in town so long after breakfast. But seeing she felt that way about it and seeing a moonlight start had its disadvantage when the other side had you outnumbered three to one. He decided it might not hurt to give them another night's lead.

As they walked off arm in arm Cup Cakes, watching from under the ice cream parlor's awning, flounced, "Men! They're all such moon calves when it comes to us women! The poor simp still thinks he's likely to get some place with that poor old maid who has to be thirty if she's been lucky!"

A fat girl who scooped servings inside came out to join her, saying, "It's freezing in back and I'm all goose-bumped. Who were you talking to just now?"

Cup Cakes replied without shame, "Myself. You see that tall specimen of male ignorance headed off to pure frustration with that old maid from the bank across the way? I just told him how to bid at that cake sale and now look where he's going!"

Her fellow ice cream wrangler suggested, "Cake sale's not until this weekend. What if he's out to screw you both?"

Cup Cakes blanched and said, "Maureen, you're awful! Who ever said I was that kind of a girl? I've never let a boy put more than a finger in me. But that's more than that handsome fool can hope for from that old maid from across the way, I'll bet!"

Chapter 12

Next morning, getting an early start and meaning it, Long-arm was invited to noon dinner at that Ranger station on the Red River. The Texas Rangers were set up like the Mex *Rurales*, or mayhaps *Los Rurales* had copied the older Anglo organization, complete with regulation Colt .45 Model '73 sixguns designated "Army" with a seven and a half inch barrel or "Peacemaker" when the barrel was four and three-quarter-inches. After that Texas Rangers wore white shirts instead of *rurale* gray and their new badges looked like silver stars in a silver circle instead of the silver coins they'd worn before they were disbanded for a spell after riding for the Confederacy.

They mostly worked alone out of stations described as barracks and looking more like railroad stops where no rails ran. The one at the junction of the Wichita and Red served the sort of grub you'd expect at a cattle camp run by a decent boss. So that noon the menu called for Anglo biscuits and gravy with Mex *frijoles* and *chil con carne*. The coffee Arbuckle Brand, of course.

Arbuckle Coffee was roasted and ground ingenious in a manner to brew drinkable over a camp fire, in a can if need be. So like cow hands, the Texas Rangers turned up their noses at brands selling for more but needing to be brewed in confounded contraptions.

As he dined with four Rangers at a deal table out back in a recently swept and watered down brick patio, Longarm brought the Rangers up to date on his mission. They were interested but not excited. Like Scotland Yard over in England, the Texas Rangers left such matters to the local law until they were called in on a case. Once they were, as in the case of Scotland Yard, things got more professional, since the Rangers, like Scotland Yard inspectors, were trained peace officers rather than lawmen chosen by the county or township courthouse gangs.

Since Longarm made no formal request for help, which would have had to come with a federal court order, they sent him on his way full of black coffee up the downright dusty trail to the panhandle.

The infernal coating of dust, fine as a whore's face powder, offered comforting thoughts as well as uncomfortable breathing as Longarm rode with his kerchief over his face as if he might be planning to pull a holdup.

On the one hand the kerchief didn't help that much and poor Buscadero, being a horse, was in worse shape, because horses couldn't sneeze the way most critters could. Evolved for grazing and breathing at the same time, horses breathed with nostrils connected directly to their lungs and couldn't inhale through the mouth. So they could snort some but they couldn't suck air in with their mouths to shoot out their nostrils and that was why a head cold a man or his dog might barely notice could kill a horse, whilst everyone knew he could keep a horse from nickering at Indian ponies by clamping a hand across its nostrils. Nickering was more complicated than modern plumbing, if you were a horse. But Buscadero was trailing strings of dusty snot so he was probably all right, so far.

On the other more encouraging hand, all that dust, clean

104

to the horizon, would make it a bitch for any other riders to shunpike across open range away from the well-trodden trails. Longarm knew that had that delivery dray been hauled out in that barley field *after* that dust storm its path across the field would have stood out startling as a swathe of swept-off green through brownish gray.

Hungerford and his pals would have noticed this, unless they were blind, and been smart enough to stick to the riverside trail unless they were stupid.

Longarm knew they were keen-eyed and coyote cunning. So he was glad it was so dusty all about.

Trying for say forty miles by sundown, with half of it behind them on the dog-leg from the Falls to the main stream, Longarm settled into a ball breaking pace for a man whilst an easier one for a horse, by trotting a few furlongs, walking a few furlongs, and breaking trail once an hour to dismount and have a smoke with Buscadero sniffing at the roadside weeds and casting dirty looks at him.

Canteen water in the crown of his Stetson was the best he could offer, seeing horses didn't care for dust all that much.

So when they came upon a soddy where a nester in bib overalls was sweeping his pasture with a broom, Longarm reined in to ask if they might sell him some fodder and water.

The nester seemed glad he had an excuse to desist from his exercise in near futility. He called back, "Come on around to the stable, such as it is. Pump still works and not too much of New Mexico made it into our manger."

As Longarm dismounted to follow on foot, it being rude to seem more imperious than one's host, two kids backed by a woman in calico and flour-sacking apron appeared in the doorway of the soddy. The man of the spread called out, "Don't just stand there, woman! Can't you see we got company? Put some cake and coffee on the damned table in there!"

The three of them ducked as if for cover. The nester sighed and said, "She's a good old wife but she was discouraged before we woke up this morning mummified. She's stopped crying, leastways. Let's get some fodder and water in your horse."

Longarm didn't insult a country man by warning him not to fodder a horse before you watered one. He didn't ask why he saw no stock around a spread with a stable and forty acres of meadow. Had it been up to him the land office wouldn't let homesteaders file on quarter-sections of so-called farm land where it took fifteen or more acres to graze one steer to market-sized.

Leaving the watered gelding in the shady stable to munch bunchgrass hay, they went into the one room house where the pale-faced and red-eyed lady of the house served them coffee and cake as the rules of hospitality called for.

The coffe was thinner than tea and the cake came closer to what Jewish folk called *matzo*, being made the same way with unleavened flour, water and mayhaps a pinch of dust. But it was the thought that counted and Longarm pretended to enjoy a nibble, leaving some for the folk who really needed it. As they nibbled Longarm casually asked if some other riders he knew might have passed by, describing them as a couple of white boys with a gentleman of color.

They hadn't seen anything that unusual in recent memory. The nester said Captain Goodnight had some colored hands off to the panhandle but *he* hadn't seen any colored riders lately.

His woman suddenly blurted something about never seeing *nobody* in such a lonesome corner of Hell and covered her face with her apron to run outside. With her kids tagging after.

The nester stared down into his watery coffee as he murmured, "That time of the month, and all that dust."

Longarm allowed he understood and said, "I got some

distance to cover, friend. So I'd best get it on down the pike and I'd be much obliged if you'd allow me to pay you for the swell way you've taken care of us."

The nester didn't look up as he said, "No Christian expects to be paid for hospitality, mister."

Longarm said, "I know. I ain't out to insult nobody. I'd just feel better because you never invited me in off the road. I invited us in off the road and fair is fair."

The nester hopefully replied, "Well, seeing you insist."

Then his eyes got owlish as he stared down at the coin on the table between them to faintly whisper, "That's a twenty dollar double eagle, mister!"

Longarm said, "I'm sorry, friend, I ain't got anything smaller. I got lucky at cards the other night and, what the hell."

Then he got to his feet and headed out the door before the nester could say or do anything foolish.

As he'd hoped, the nester was no fool. He had a wife and kids that worried him more than vanity. So he just stood there in the doorway, tears running down both cheeks, as Longarm led Buscadero out of his stable to mount up and ride on.

He didn't look back as somebody called after him, "Goodbye, mister. Lord love you, mister!"

"Poor saps," Longarm muttered murderously, not at them but at the Office of Land Management as they rode upstream with the afternoon sun in his eyes and the kerchief back over the rest of his face. He knew Honest Abe had meant well back in '62 when he'd signed that fool Homestead Act. It had seemed a good way to settle the unsettled west a mite sooner and had the farther west been green as things were east of the Mississippi a quarter-section claim, or a hundred and sixty acres, would have added up to a handsome family farm. Everyone knew how the prosperous Pennsylvania Dutch produced tons of cheese and shoo fly pie on family farms averaging eighty acres. They just hadn't considered how tough it was to raise anything on any number of acres without expensive irrigation schemes where it averaged less than ten inches of rain a year.

Once nesters filed a homestead claim on land they'd seldom seen before they were stuck with a sort of half-ass title to their claim, they had to "Prove" it with visible construction such as sod housing and bob wire as they worked it for five years before they really owned the ground under them.

They couldn't sell an acre of homested claim that hadn't had a clear title ceded to the claimant. So many a nester had just had to walk away after putting in as much time as the French Foreign Legion asked of a desperate soul.

Interior Secretary Schurz or Little Big Eyes seemed to mean well and ran his Land Management Office as sensible as Congress would allow. But most of Congress had never been west of the Mississippi and even those who had were beholden to the powerful cattlemen's associations or the just as unreasonable Grange Movement, each with its own axe to grind and both clouding up and raining over any elected official who dared to suggest Land Tenure and Riperian rights based on Old Country Common Law, based in turn on Ancient Roman Tradition, might not always work west of say Latitude 100°.

He could only hope the starvlings back yonder would use the little he could spare to get to town and scout up a more profitable position. A saloon swamper made more take-home pay than your average nester.

As he rode ever westward the dust all around still lay all around, but not as thick, as the river to his right ran betwixt ever higher banks the land north and south of it rose, and dust tended to settle *down* more than it settled up.

But it had still been a dry dusty day in the saddle when they rode into the riverside settlement of Naseca and Longarm confided to his mount. "Buscadero, old pal, I would say we have gone just about fucking far enough for one day!"

The chestnut, who was now more mustard-colored, gave him no argument. The livery near the well-traveled trail was run by Indians. Neither Longarm not Buscadero cared. He never asked if they were Cado or Comanche as they took kindly charge of his mount and promised to clean him off with damp burlap that wouldn't raise dust around his head. He suspected Naseca had to be an Indian name, since it wasn't Spanish. But asking what it meant would have been the same as asking them their nation and this could be a touchy subject in West Texas where the Cado, related to the Pawnee, had been friendly Indians eager to play Cowboy whilst the Comanche had been more inclined to play Cowboys and Indians. Since the Buffalo War they'd lost in the mid '70s the Comanche had started to play Cowboy, too, and some were good at it.

He mosied across the way and treated himself to a tub bath and a warm set down meal at the one hotel cum trail-break before, feeling a whole lot better, he bellied up to the bar of the Naseca Saloon to discover they served what, if it wasn't ice cold, they could lace with Maryland rye.

Once he got to jawing with the regulars Longarm discovered Naseca was Comanche for mullberries growing alongside the Red and that nobody looking at all like the distinctive trio he was after had been by before him. So he muttered, "This must be the place" and scouted up their local law, a semi-official constable who seemed impressed when Longarm flashed a badge and that warrant from Judge Parker.

The constable, a skinny old cuss called Winslow, asked how they meant to trap those three desperados. Seeing he only had a couple kid deputies.

Longarm explained, "Don't need to trap 'em. Don't care if they ride on through, long as I know they did or did not. I'm working on whether they've already made it out to take shelter with another suspect or they're still on their way. I don't *want* to try to stop them *here*. If I do I'm likely to have to shoot one or more of them and dead men can't talk. I just parted company with such an uncooperative witness back in Wichita Falls. So I want to pay out more line in hopes of reeling in the bigger fish who paid for all this confusion. I'd like to have him tell us why he did it, once I make sure he won't do it again."

Constable Winslow wasn't slow as he looked, hardly anybody could have been. He said, "Then all you need from me and mine is extra eyes. We don't have to even howdy those white boys and that darky as we merely note their passage. But where will you be?"

Longarm said, "Over to the saloon for a spell and then slugabed at the hotel for a year or so. I'll be obliged if somebody wakes me when and if. I frankly ain't betting the farm on it. I'm just eliminating."

They shook on it and Longarm went back to bullshit with the boys along the bar. He was tempted by talk about a friendly little game in the backroom. That double eagle he'd parted with had been two weeks' pay for a top hand. But it was tough to come out ahead in an honest game and Naseca didn't seem a town to nourish professional card sharks.

Thanks to long ago pillow talk with more than one sporting lady and a stage magician, cheating card sharks were the only players he cared to buck. That saw saying you can't cheat an honest man was on the money.

So he nursed his schooner, swapped yarns, and having satisfied himself Naseca was a right dull town, he was fixing to turn in when Rube Shire came in, dusty as hell and looking beat.

Half staggering over to the bar as Longarm signalled for a beer on the double, Rube Shire said, "I was hoping to catch up with you. I think I've hurt myself. I rode after you to tell you about that darky."

Longarm blinked, "Artistic Algernon? They caught him back yonder?"

Rube Shire shook his head and said, "Not hardly. They *found* him. Kids hunting crawdads along the Wichita. Found him half in and half out of the water. Shot in the back, the same as Lawyer Lovecraft, with what Doc Ballard suspects is the same Navy .36."

As Longarm digested that, Shire explained, "Ain't many unconverted Navy cap and balls around. Doc says the slug in the darky never came from any brass cartridge."

Longarm said, "I know how a coroner reads bullets. The question before the house is where do we go from here?"

Chapter 13

Rube Shire frowned and said, "Don't you mean to ride back with me? I told Sheriff Maguire I'd fetch you!"

"Why?" asked Longarm, gathering up both beer schooners to steer Rube to a corner table as he said, "Maquire knows Jackson's dead and Doc Ballard is better than me at autopsies. Do they need me to come all the way to tell 'em why that colored rider was likely shot in the back?"

Rube said, "They wanted to get rid of him, same reasons they wanted to rid themselves of Lawyer Lovecraft. Two ragged-ass white riders don't attract as much attention out our way."

Longarm sat Rube at a table, took a seat across from him, and said, "There you go. Hungerford's a sweet kid. He used Artistic Algernon and that delivery dray to where they might stand out and got rid of them like smoked-down cigar butts. I wonder if the Tinker Kid has noticed that or not. In either case after the three of them got rid of a local who likely fixed them up with fresh mounts, a change of duds and so on, the two white boys had no use for the ball and chain Jackson would prove in mostly white cow country. If they left him down the Wichita any distance they'd

113

have had no call to go back to town. They'd have rid on. Has Doc estimated a time for Jackson's death?"

Rube reached for his beer as he said, "Not long after Lawyer Lovecraft. Darky had commenced to relax when they hauled him out of the shallows."

Longarm said, "Try her this way. Say Hungerford and the Tinker Kid gunned the two of them shortly after meeting up with Lovecraft and put the two of them in that delivery dray. We're talking before midnight. They had to haul all that evidence out of town before that unexpected duster. They dumped Jackson in the shallows along the way and drove on to run Lovecraft and that dray out in that barley field. They wanted both to be found."

Rube swallowed, sighed in satisfaction and asked, "How come?"

Longarm said, "Stage magicians call that misdirection. They wanted us interested in where they *wasn't*."

He stuck a pose and ponificated, "Blessed are they who run around like chickens with their heads cut off because they're likely to see about as much as chickens with their heads cut off. But as I see it, they rode on down to the Red to head either way before we ever found Lawyer Lovecraft and by now I've just set up a roadblock that may do some kid deputies some good as training. If they rode west toward the Lazy S or your trail town of Singer's Wells there is no way in hell to catch up with them on the trail. Time I get there they'll have taken cover or ridden on west into the cow thief country of North-East New Mexicao Territory."

Rube Shire sipped more suds, sighed, and said, "Well, I'll tell the sheriff I tried. Soon as I rest up a mite and wrangle me a fresh mount to head back on."

Longarm shook his head and said, "I thought you said you meant to be a lawman when you grew up?"

The former rider for the Reconstuction scowled and said, "I'll have you know I was a sergeant in the Texas State Police one time!"

Longarm soothed, "That was then and this is now. A full time lawman like a professional soldier learns to apply himself to a steady job. The crooks, like the enemy, will be there in the morning and you'll do a better job on either after a night's rest and a solid breakfast. That's how come Soldier Blue keeps beating Mister Lo. Indians I've talked to about it say it drove them crazy. Born warriors get all lathered up to go whooping and slashing and shooting until they're worn down to nubs and then the pokey army slowly but surely rounds them up and takes all their guns away. Are you listening to me, Rube?"

Shire nodded soberly.

Longarm said, "You've rid yourself into the ground. You have to be more tired than me and I just spent a long dusty day in the saddle. If you overnight here and head back after a good breakfast in the morning on a fresh mount, you'll get there soon enough. Neither Lawyer Lovecraft nor Artistic Algernon are going anyplace, whilst Hungerford and the Tinker Kid are likely long gone."

Rub Shire sipped more suds with more color to his cheeks as he told Longarm, "I follow your drift. I'm riding on the Singer's Wells with you. I know the country better than you and you'll need us to back your play if those rascals have holed up around the Lazy S."

"Us?" asked Longarm.

Shire said, "I told you. I have hands working for me on both bases. Couple of boys at my lumberyard have asked if they can be my deputies when I'm the sheriff out yonder."

"What about that ice plant you have up for sale in The Falls?" asked Longarm.

Rube Shire said, "Like you said, it'll still be there, and can you see the claim I'll have on the office of Sheriff if I help a famous lawman catch two famous outlaws!"

Longarm said, "Only Hungerford is famous. The Tinker Kid still wants to be. But I admire young gents with ambition. I thought you were a public-spirited cuss just helping the law out for the hell of it."

Rube Shire laughed boyishly as he looked off into the distance from under the brim of that *rurale* sombrero. He said, "If only you knew how ambitious I've always been, and how all the pretty bubbles I've blown have just popped in my face. It's the *almost* making it big that galls me so, Longarm. Time after time I've thought I had the answer and time after time . . . you wouldn't understand."

Longarm said, "Sure I would. You want to end up rich and famous."

Rube sighed and said, "I'd settle for comfortable. You mind that old Jewish vaudeville joke about the old gent knocked down by a brewery wagon?"

Longarm allowed he wasn't familiar with that one.

Shire said, "Crowd gathers around the old gent. Somebody puts a rolled up coat under his head, tells him they've sent for a doc and asks him if he's comfortable. So the old gent smiles up at them to say, '*Nu*, I make a living.'"

Longarm chuckled at the picture. Rube said, "That's all I want out of this game I never asked to join. I want to be *comfortable*. I want just enough wealth and importance to feel I don't have to take shit off anybody. Don't it gall you, taking shit off everybody?"

Longarm said, "I don't have to take shit off *everybody*. We all have to take shit off *somebody*. Queen Victoria has to stick her tongue out and say 'Ah!' when her sawbones tells her to, and how would you like to be married up with Lemonade Lucy Hayes, who won't abide hard liquor nor cigar smoke at White House dinners?"

Rube said, "I don't mean shit a man can laugh off. I mean the galling take-it-or-leave-it shit a man has to take off his boss if he's a working man or his customers if he thinks he's working for himself. Just once I'd like to smile right back at a smug-eye and tell him I aim to leave it.

Can't you just see that smug smile fade as he sees he never had you over that barrel after all?"

Shire shook his head wearily and said, "It's not being over a barrel I mind as much as the cocksuckers feeling so certain they *have* you over a barrel!"

Longarm quietly said, "I'm tempted to introduce you to a soul mate back at The Falls who will go on about the pangs of mediocrity. You got a lot in common. You piss and moan about elusive goals instead of counting your blessings. I met a gent earlier today who'd cut off his own right arm to be in your boots, you poor mediocre cuss!"

Rube Shire insisted he just wanted to feel comfortable.

Longarm let it go. He knew Rube didn't want to hear how few money hungry gents ever felt comfortable. No matter how much they got they wanted more and ever more until in the end they died and left it all to women who were likely glad to see the last of 'em. Longarm had heard as much during more than one pillow conversation with a rich widow.

But at least he got Rube Shire calmed down enough to ride on with him at a sensible pace after a good night's sleep and that hearty breakfast.

They got to know one another and like one another better as they rode ever higher, westward, into the panhandle. It took more time than anyone would take to relate it all in tedious detail. But four days after he'd left Wichita Falls Longarm found himself in Singer's Wells with his old pard, Rube.

By then Longarm could see why Rube found himself spread thin with enterprises out that way and back near the edges of civilizatuon. It made more sense for Big Dutch Steinmuller to stay at his nearby spread and send flunkies off to Fort Worth or Fort Smith to cater to his rich whims. Longarm wondered if Big Dutch knew he needed a new lawyer yet. The imperious cattle king had a good alibi

117

whether he did or didn't. So how was Big Dutch fixing to feel about the hand he'd sent to save Hungerford's neck paying them both back by back shooting Lovecraft?

Or had that been another whim of Big Dutch Steinmuller's?

Either way, nobody seemed to know who the Singer they'd named Singer's Wells after might be. The wells were natural sinkholes on the outskirts of the settlement. Nobody drew water from them. They were said to be contaminated with dead buffalo, dead cattle and worse. Old-timers said "Singer" had derived from the Comanche "Sito" meaning piss. Any white man who'd been in the panhandle as long as an army hitch qualified as an old-timer.

After that Singers's Wells drew its water from regular bore wells sunk in the locally high water table and seemed small for a town but bigger than Longarm had expected, jawing along the way with a cuss who owned most of what there was.

Rube Shire had been modest. His lumber yard covered a city block, his feed store rivaled the general store in size and Shire had confided he was out to buy it so'd he could incorporate the post office in the back into his own holdings and be the local postmaster. He'd said he wasn't married up yet. But at the rate he was going he was likely to leave a rich widow pouting that he'd never paid enough attention to *her*, the uncaring brute.

When word got around Rube was back in town Longarm half-expected a brass band to show up and back all the well wishers. You'd have thought he'd just come back from the war. The Trojan War. He'd said he's been working on getting popular out that way.

As Rube held court in the saloon he held half-interest in, their horses having been spirited away by devotees, he asked and was given assurances no strangers of any description had shown up around Singer's Wells since Spring Roundup and none of the hands riding in off the Range had seemed all that strange. Longarm agreed with Rube that nobody in town before Hungerford's escape could have been Hungerford. It remained to be seen if the Tinker Kid had ever passed through. Lawyer Lovecraft had to have known him from somewhere.

Longarm told the pal who seemed to own the place, "The mount who got me this far ain't in shape to carry me farther, Rube. Could you fix me up with a ride on out to the Lazy S?"

Rube Shire said, "You can't be serious! It's getting on toward sundown. Let us put you up here for the night and I'll ride out with you in the morning. Big Dutch ain't there and they say his housekeeper, Miss Fraw Lion, is sort of unpredictable. You'll want somebody backing your play out yonder."

Longarm turned to call out, "Anybody here willing to hire me a horse for the evening? I got my own bridle and saddle."

Shire said, "Aw, for Pete's sake, I'll loan you one of my ponies."

So Longarm rode into the sunset with the same saddle and saddle gun aboard a black pony called Tocuehtucan, which was Comanche for midnight. Rube said they still had assimilated Indians trading in horseflesh out on the panhandle.

The panhandle was sort of a northward extension of the staked plains, so-called because when you approached 'em from the south there was this bodacious escarpment that made the plains on a higher lever look as if they were up on stakes or pilings of eroded subsoil. Beyond the sudden elevation the *llanos* or plains rolled more like a wave-tossed sea of grass than the word "plains" described. So as many a ranger or cavalry patrol had long since discovered, you could lose things behind a grassy swell or sometimes a damned deep wash aspiring to becoming a canyon.

Hence Longarm wasn't surprised when he suddenly

came upon a lamp-lit window agaimt the dark horizon back-lit by the setting sun and in no time at all he was riding down this gentle slope towards what really did resemble a baron's castle rising from the prairie sod as more of the same.

Dogs barked and Mex kids yelled as he rode in. Then a tall she-male figure was outlined by lamplight in a suddenly flung open door and when Longarm reined in and dismounted she yelled at a Mex kid in High Dutch.

It seemed to work when you trained Mex kids right. They led his mount around to the back as the woman in the doorway called, "We have you been expecting. Come. You will some hot chocolate have and then we will talk."

That sounded fair. At closer range she was about forty and she'd likely been a looker in her day. Her blond hair was worn in a tight bun and her slender figure was uncertain in a chin-to-insteps outfit that matched the Comanche pony he'd just dismounted from.

As he joined her, doffing his hat, she said she was Fraulein Helga. This didn't surprise Longarm much.

He followed her inside. She waved him to a tufted leather sofa in front of a cold baronial fireplace and yelled in High Dutch for what sounded like *schokolade*. When you yelled anything in that tone of voice even Mexicans seemed to understand you.

Longarm tried to show her his badge and I.D. She remained on her feet as she told she'd just said she'd been expecting him.

As they waited he asked her who'd told her he was coming. She sniffed and said, "I needed by nobody to be told. I knew so soon as I heard somebody like you they would send."

A scared-looking Mex gal came in with his hot chocolate and some un-glazed donuts on a tray. She placed them on the low slung rosewood table betwixt the sofa and the fireplace and crawfished out before Fraulein Helga could swallow her. The frosty housskeepr said, "You may if you wish to dunk."

So Longarm did. Donuts dipped in hot chocolate tasted swell. So he went on dunking and sipping as he said her boss, Mine Herr Steinmuller, had told him he could look around out there.

Fraulein Helga said, "That is a lie. We both better know. But now you are about to die, *so es macht nichts*."

Longarm stared up at her, stared down at the chocolate he'd been sipping, and muttered, "Aw, you didn't!"

But he figured she must have as he tried to rise and wound up falling down and down into darkness that seemed to have no bottom to it.

Chapter 14

Longarm hadn't noticed he was naked as a jay when he came in from that dust storm but there was nothing he could do about it before he got his tweed suit out of that overnighter in the baggage room. And so hoping nobody in the waiting room would notice he went on over to claim it but Miss Cup Cakes behind the counter said they only had three flavors and when she fetched it from the shelf it wasn't an overnight bag at all. It looked more like a great big cake zebra striped with chocolate and vanilla icing.

He said, "I don't never eat chocolate, Miss Cup Cakes. It's poison." She pouted, "I baked it special for you and I'm twelve years old and I want you to marry up with me so there!"

He said, "I can't marry up with no twelve-year-olds, I got to get Famous Frank back to Denver and come to study on it, wasn't Famous Frank with me when I first came in here, Miss Cup Cakes?"

She said, "Hear me, drink some more!" and he said, "I can't. It tasted like bitter chocolate and I fear I'm about to puke again!"

Then Miss Cup Cakes was holding his head whilst he threw up everything he'd ever eaten since he was twelve years old and he kept trying to wake up but no matter how he tried he was still stark naked and he couldn't stop puking.

Then he saw he lay naked on his side in ruby light with his head in Miss Cup Cake's lap whilst she wiped the vomit off his face with a cool damp rag and a gentle touch.

The rest of him lay on corn husk bedding and Miss Cup Cakes smelled of love grass smoke and buckskin as she set the rag aside and held more black-drink to his lips, murmuring, "Drink. You have not thrown up enough."

Longarm answered, "Yes I have and who are you, ma'am? I don't recall you in this dream before."

Then, as he rolled over enough to stare up into sloe eyes black as midnight he asked the Indian lady holding his head who she was and how he'd gotten there.

She called out, "Hey, Rube? He's awake now!"

So Rube Shire joined them in what seemed a smoke house lit by one candle to hunker down beside them in his creaky leather charro pants and say, "Howdy. Thought you were a gonner for a time, there. But we knew if anybody could fix you up it would be Miss Sunny Person, here. She's a *puha* in spite of her looks."

Suddenly more aware of his naked state, Longarm sat up and crossed his legs to conceal his charms and get a better look at Miss Sunny Person, who turned out to be, as he got to know her better, a right handsome young lady in a beaded buckskin Comanche *kwasu*.

Rube Shire said, "We got there as they were digging a hole for you out back. One of Miss Fraw Lion's greasers told one of my greasers all she'd just done to a Gringo inside. When we busted in you were still breathing. So we draped you over a saddle and loped back to town with you. Sent for Miss Sunny Person, here, and like I said, she's a *puha*."

"She's supposed to be at Fort Sill, too. But let's talk about Fraulein Helga."

Rube replied, "She got away. Must have lit out with

124

them outlaws she was harboring as we rode in. We only rode in because after you'd left I got to brooding about what a spooky old gal she was and, as you just found out, I was right. So I possed up some of my hands to ride out to the Lazy S and make sure you were all right. The rest you know."

Longarm asked the Comanche lady, "Could I have my jeans back and does the B.I.A. know you're here, Miss Sunny Person?"

She laughed, it startled him some, and said, "I only wear this outfit when I'm calling on *Tataco* for guidance. They did not make all of us go to Fort Sill. Those of us who could claim *taibo* blood and knew how to behave ourselves were allowed to remain where we belonged. One of my grandmother's was a *taibo* captive. When I am not in tribal dress most take me for *Yuutaibo*, I mean Mexican."

"Might *puha* have the same meaning as the Mex word, *bruja?*" Longarm asked as she handed him his jeans, observing, "You don't want your underwear anymore."

As he hauled them on she continued, "A *bruja* or witch thinks her powers come from evil spirits. We never talk to evil spirits. The good spirits sometimes talk to our old ones and they in turn tell us which parts of which things might be good medicine. When Rube told me you had been poisoned I knew you needed black-drink. I know you think you are better, now, but hear me, you are not. You must rest and stay out of the sun for a time while I feed you things to make you strong and watch for signs that poison she served you might be coming back. I know the root she wrung that poison out of. I could smell it in your vomit. I did not know any *taibo* women knew about such things. She must have been talking to Mexicans."

Rube Shire said, "I figure she's headed downstream with Hungerford and the Tinker Kid. I was hoping Miss Sunny Person, here, would say you were fit to ride with

125

me. Since you ain't, I reckon I'll have to make do with some of my own riders."

"You're going after them? How do you know she's with Hungerford and The Kid?" asked Longarm.

Rube said, "Got to go after 'em. Somebody has to. Nobody signed no guest book out to the Lazy S but some of the Mexican help, with her out of earshot, said two Gringo boys, one pimple-faced and the other just smirky, were hiding in the next room whilst Miss Fraw Lion served you poison. Mex gal who says she never wanted to bring it from the kitchen says the fox-faced one, she likely meant Hungerford, wanted to just gun you and be done with it, but Miss Fraw Lion was a caution about keeping things tidy and insisted there be no blood all over the place. So . . . I got to get it on down the road, Longarm. They already have a fair lead on us and you'll be all right with Miss Sunny Person, here. So I'll be on my way."

Suiting actions to his words, he sprang to his feet and lit out as Longarm struggled to rise, shouting, "Wait for me! Where's my gun? I want my gun, Dad blast it!"

Sunny Person pressed him back down on the corn husks, soothing, "I have your gun and everything else upstairs. We are in the root cellar of my shop because I knew you were going to shit and vomit a lot. The black-drink gets the poison out of you that way. Be still and wait until we see if you want to shit or vomit some more. If you do not we can go upstairs and I will make you strong with beef broth and fresh baked *tohtia*. Maybe coffee, if you can keep it down."

He insisted, "I got to ride with Rube! That's my prisoner he's going after without me!"

She soothed, "Do you want him captured or do you want him to ride on, laughing, with you down on your hands and knees behind him? Rube will catch them. He used to be a lawman and he has eight riders with him. All nine of them are strong enough for a good fight. You are

126

not strong enough to mount a horse without help. Why are you acting like a spoiled child who won't let anyone else share his toys?"

Longarm smiled sheepishly and said, "I've heard it described to me as the male ego. You're right, of course. I still feel like somebody dragged me through the keyhole backward and, say, how did I get this clean if you say I was . . . you know?"

She said, "Oh, I had to change those corn husks under you more than once, too. I had them undress you before I gave you the black-drink. I knew what it was going to do to you. Once you lay there naked on corn husks I only had to wipe you down with wet rags every few minutes until you'd purged the poison. The last few times you mostly shit or puked water. So it wasn't so bad."

He said he was sorry and managed not to ask a dumb question. It was obvious she'd been washing off his privates as he shit his fool self. He tried to think of her as a doctor. It wasn't easy. Seeing how few doctors practiced in beaded buckskin after a smoke bath, even when they were gals of say thirty with smoldering eyes and yards of shiny black hair hanging down in braids.

She asked if he wanted his duds, boots and guns, seeing he went on trying to get up. He felt less light-headed by the time he'd dressed to go upstairs. But he still reeled some and she had to steady him a time or two as she helped him up the cellar steps with that candle in her free hand.

At the top of the stairs they found themselves in a surprisingly modern kitchen with painted cabinets and a handsome cast iron range fresh-dressed with stove blacking. When he commented she told him Rube Shire had built her place and others like it the length of her city block. He sensed it might sound mean-spirited if he asked if there was anything Rube Shire might not be up to. So he never did. He knew he had no call to ask how else old Rube might serve her and he wasn't certain he cared to know.

Sunny Person asked why he was smiling like so as she sat him down at her kitchen table.

He said, "I must be getting better. My mind has commenced to run in familiar channels again. You say this is some sort of shop you got up here, Miss Sunny Person?"

As she poked the banked fire in her range awake the assimilated Comanche breed said, "Medicine. What you might call a drugstore if your kind of drugstore sold my kind of medicine. A lot of *Yuutaibo*, what you call Mexicans, are not really Mexicans and some of those who are from that far away feel more certain about the old cures. Comanche and Nahuatl, you say Aztec, are sister tongues."

Longarm allowed he'd noticed that. Next to the more familiar Algonquin most white folk thought of as "Indian" the far-flung Ho or Uto-Aztec lingo was spoken by thrice as many Indians, from the Great Basin down to Nicaragua on both slopes of the Continental Divide. This other gal he knew, a white gal attached to that Museum in Denver, had told him the professors thought the far-flung and adaptable bunch had started as Digger Indians in the Nevada desert, picking up any useful notions as they expanded in all directions to wind up peaceful Hopi, blood-thirsty Aztec and so on, including the original Horse Indians, the Comanche. He knew from unauthorized visits south of the border that the old Spanish had only *thought* they'd wiped out or converted the Aztec. Albeit most Mexicans might call Sunny Person a *curada* or good witch.

As she got the fire going to reheat the broth she'd made earler Longarm blinked, shook his head to clear it and said, "I sure wish I could wake up all the way! I just now noticed the sun seems to be shining outside. It was setting when I got out to the Lazy S. Was I really off in dreamland all night long?"

She laughed softly and said, "The sun will soon be going down again. Didn't you know that was why Rube was beside himself as we waited to see if you would live? That wicked woman and those two bad boys have almost a full day's lead on Rube, now. They say he's good, but I don't know."

Longarm whistled and said, "That root juice she put in that chocolate must have been something else!"

She said, "It was. It should have killed you. But you are big and strong and Rube says you spilled a lot of the chocolate she served you."

"I reckon they thought I was dead if they were digging me a grave out back," Longarm observed.

Sunny Person said, "I don't think they cared if you were dead or not."

He nodded soberly and said, "You're right. She sure was wicked, as tidy as she might have been."

A few minutes later he was dunking *tohtia* in beef broth and enjoying both like hell. Comanche-baked corn bread looked and tasted like Mex *tortillas*, which wasn't hard to figure when you considered their Aztec cousins had taught Spanish-speaking folk to bake *tortillas*.

Tamales were an Aztec word and notion, too. The way he's heard it, down Mexico way, if you had one drop of Spanish blood in you you were Spanish, if you were pure Indian on both sides you allowed folk to call you Mexican and if anybody called you *Indio* he'd have a fight on his hands unless he was a whole lot bigger than you.

When a Mexican called another Mexican an Indian he meant an uneducated country boy. In Longarm's opinion, there was a lot to be said for the Spanish approach to the Indian Problem. It might have been tougher on some at first, but they'd saved a whole lot of time and expenses down Mexico way by just telling everybody they were Spanish subjects who'd best put on a pair of pants and show up for High Mass come Sunday or they'd wind up dead.

Some few quill Indians such as the Yaqui still followed their old way in the wilder hills of Mexico, but a heap of folk who'd still behave like Apache, Comanche, Lakota or such had they grown up north of the border thought they were church-going Mexicans down yonder.

Even after Sunny Person had ducked out of the kitchen to change into a cotton blouse and calico skirt she still smelled of her smoke bathing and likely *felt* Indian in spite of being a quarter-white. They said Crazy Horse had had blue eyes and light brown hair he never let anybody photograph, but he'd gone down fighting as an untamed Lakota. It sure beat all how the way folk *felt* seemed to count more than what they might really *be*.

After he'd put away a second helping of bread and broth along with black coffee that stayed down with no second thought Longarm felt a lot better. But he took his good time gathering up his belongings and felt steady on his legs as he strapped on his sixgun.

Sunny Person let him get that far before she asked what he thought he was doing.

He said, "Got to find old Buscadero, saddle up and ride. If we push it a tad we might catch up with Rube and his boys this side of Wichita Falls and I saw Frank Hungerford and the Tinker Kid *first*!"

She said, "Hear me! You almost died. You should not try to go anyplace for at least a few days!"

Longarm found his Stetson, put it on, and said, "I know you mean well and I'm much obliged for all you've done. But I got to scout up my horse and get going, Miss Sunny Person."

She followed after him, muttering to herself in Comanche, as Longarm opened the kitchen door and stepped out on her porch in the late afternoon sunlight.

Then he seemed to be spread on his back in the dust at the foot of her back porch steps as she stood over him with an I-Told-You-So look in her black sloe eyes.

So Longarm muttered, "Well, shit, I reckon I'd best give it a day or so after all."

Chapter 15

So they sat on her porch steps at the close of the day, sharing a cheroot as a cricket off in the rabbit bushes got to chirping. She called it a *twataki* and she told him how come she'd come back to her home range from that swell new reservation in the Indian Territory.

She said, "I could not breathe there. The air was heavy. Like soup. You had to suck and suck to take a breath. I was not the only one there who thought Little Big Eyes was trying to suffocate us. I know they said the grass grew greener there but I could not stay. You would not understand."

Longarm understood. Having acclimated to the altitude of Denver on up, he'd tried to explain to other whites during that reservation jump by seemingly wrong-headed Dull Knife that the unsettled politicians back in Washington thought those gasping Cheyenne were just being Mister Lo when they pissed and moaned they couldn't live on what Washington felt to be perfectly fine well-watered prairie, a tad nicer than the High Plains they'd been raising Ned on to the north-west. The Indians themselves had felt confused as to what felt so awful about resevation land they called a harsh and hostile desert, infested with timbered draws and prairie sod thicker than the sod folk built houses out of in dried country.

Dull Knife and his band hadn't understood they were suffering from altitude sickness. They'd only known their hearts felt heavy in their breasts so they had to get away from there. Going from thicker to thinner air felt the opposite. Your head felt lighter and your heart beat faster for the days or months it took you to get used to different air pressure.

By the time those literally homesick Cheyenne had made it halfway home winter and the U.S. Cav was upon them. They'd scared the wits out of Little Big Eyes, or Interior Secretary Schurz, an otherwise reasonable cuss, by appearing to act so unreasonable.

Considering that confusion, Longarm felt more inclined to go along with Sunny Person's prescribed treatment calling for plenty of liquids, ever more solid foods and plenty of rest.

They talked about this and that and he managed to establish Sunny Person and Rube Shire were no more than friends. She admired him and said she'd vote for him if only Indians or women of any complexion were allowed to vote and he was running for Sheriff in an incorporated county.

So later, when she suggested they get to bed in as natural a way as they'd been there before, Longarm found his spirit was willing but his flesh was still weak. So Sunny Person got on top, Indian style, as free and easy as if she'd been expecting to for some time.

After they'd climaxed, sort of casually but with great satisfaction, she confessed she had been planning his ruination ever since she'd first washed off his old organ grinder down in the cellar. The poison had made him hard as a rock, as if his neck had been broken. He felt no call to observe that old saw about hanged men was true. They shit their pants with a hard-on, just as if they'd been poisoned.

He didn't ask where she'd learned to screw Indian style, seeing she was an Indian old enough to know what she was doing.

Sob sisters who didn't seem to know much about *white* men were forever going on about how Indian men abused their women. Reservation Indians living on the white man's handouts as they drank too much and ran to fat sometimes beat their women. Quill Indians who counted coup and sported scalps they'd collected themselves considered it cowardly to hit women or children. They counted it manly to walk up to a grizzly and punch it in the nose. But they'd let a woman fuss at them or abide kids poking them with sticks as if they didn't notice. And the funny thing was, their kids grew up obedient and respectful as most others.

Indian women walked behind their men on the trail and got on top in bed for the same practical consideration whites showed when they expected the man to walk on the curb side betwixt his lady fair and splashed up horse shit. An Indian walking out front was inclined to spot a snake in the grass or a lurking enemy first, whilst getting on top saved wear and tear of the she-male tailbone where everybody slept on the ground.

Sunny Person slept in a feather bed, but he could tell by the way she planted her bare feet atop the matress she'd been broken in in an old-fashioned *kaani*, which was close as a Comanche got to a wigwam.

The next morning he saddled up Buscadero and rode over to Singer's famous stinky holes in the ground and when the smell made him reel in the saddle he cantered back without falling off, but agreeing with Sunny Person he wasn't ready for that long ride back to The Falls yet.

So his recovery passed no more tediously than a soldier's seventy-two hour pass, shacked up. They both enjoyed the evenings more, once he was up to getting on top and taking charge and during the lazy days he got to know the folk around Singer's Wells and obtain a better grasp on the situation out to the Lazy S.

Nobody seemed upset by the absence of Fraulein Helga. Nobody in town had liked her, albeit opinions varied as to whether she'd been a servant, a mistress or kin to Big Dutch. Nobody knew anything about Hungerford or the Tinker Kid. There was no way to wire for information out at The Wells.

So on the third day he rose and like it or not rode east on his well-rested chestnut barb and if it killed him it killed him.

It didn't kill him, he just found the long lonesome days on the trail tedious as hell. Buscadero was a tough old horse and Longarm was an experienced rider who knew how to get a tad more out of a mount without hurting it than your average cavalry officer.

After that, the cavalry needed reserve energy in a mount by the time they got their fustest with the mostest. The regulation thirty mile *etape* was meant to allow for unexpected action along the way or after you got there. Knowing you'd be stopping for the night at a wayside rest where there'd be water, fodder, and a safe stall to leave him in allowed Longarm to push for closer to fifty miles a day. But he could still see why Big Dutch and Rube made the trip as seldom as possible.

He and Buscadero were half way there, stopped for the night where Texas no longer spanned the Red River to their north, when he met up with Big Dutch and his bunch coming the other way.

The meeting took place in the saloon across from the livery Longarm had just tucked Buscadero away in. After a long tense moment as Longarm saw what he'd walked in to, the cattle king holding court at a corner table waved him in, saying, "We heard. Ran into Rube Shire down the Red, headed the other way. Fortunately for you, Rube's a

134

friend of mine. So I believe Helga tried to do you dirty. Now suppose you tell me how come."

Longarm sat down, accepted the beer Mister Horn pulled out of thin air for him and honestly replied, "Ain't certain. I barely spoke to the lady before I was being treated for chocolate poisoning by another lady. Rube tells me he was told she was hiding out those outlaws I've been after. Did he tell you about Lawyer Lovecraft and that colored rider?"

Big Dutch nodded soberly and said, "He did. I don't see how Helga could have murdered either, any more than I could have."

Longarm nodded and agreed, "The both of you have alibis I'd hate to have to crack in court. The same can't be said for Hungerford or the Tinker Kid. They only needed a short lead on Rube and me to beat us out to The Wells and run home to Momma Helga."

Big Dutch said, "Helga never had no kids. She was never married. I doubt she was ever kissed by any mortal man."

He sipped some suds and mused, "That might have been what ailed her. I'm a man and she was a woman and there were times, over the years she worked for me, but I never. A man who trifles with his help is asking for more trouble than Ellen Terry with a certificate of virginity would be worth."

Longarm said he'd drink to that and did so before he asked in a desperately casual voice just what position Fraulein Helga had held out to the Lazy S.

Big Dutch said, "Housekeeper. Ran the house for me because I had no other lady of the house."

He stared down into his suds as he soberly added, "Marriage don't seem to agree with me. First wife ran off on me during the war whilst I was riding for Texas. Got the letter from her as I was nursing a leg wound after Chickamagua.

Accused me of thinking more of Texas than I did of her. She may have been right, looking back. I was bitter at the time."

He sipped, shrugged and said, "Second wife, down on the Brazos, was easier to get along with. So we had a few good years and then she up and died of the yellowjack. The docs told me she'd been in a family way when the fever took her. I figured the Good Lord had to be telling me something, so I concentrated more on getting rich after that. I hired poor Helga partly as a favor to friends of my elders, from their old country. Helga was a poor relation who couldn't seem to hold a job on this side of the pond. As you likely noticed, her English was odd and her manners were abrupt. You're the first visitor she ever tried to murder, though. Poor old gal must have gone loco. Can't help feeling a little guilty about that. Might have helped if I had screwed her now and again. There were nights out to the spread when I suspected she wanted me to do *something* to her. But I reckon we're just as well off without her. House may wind up a mess, but dead bodies buried out back ain't neat, neither."

Longarm broke out his notebook and asked if Big Dutch would mind giving him the name of Fraulein Helga's Texas kin.

Big Dutch shook his head and said, "I don't have a dog in that fight. Old Helga may be loco. She may be harboring fugitives. But she'd never wronged me or mine and you're still breathing. So catch her if you can but you'll get no help from this child!"

Longarm allowed he understood and asked where Big Dutch and his bunch had met up with Rube Shire and that other bunch.

Big Dutch seemed to have had second thoughts about leveling with the law, judging from the way he replied, "On the trail, like I said. I disremember where. By this time Rube's in Wichita Falls, where he'll have cut the trail off

Helga and them boys or lost it. I hope he's lost it. I ain't about to take sides either way, you understand, but I've almost fucked Fraulein Helga more than once and them boys mean nothing to me neither way."

Longarm said, "They're killers. They killed your own lawyer. The one you sent to Fort Smith to defend Famous Frank!"

The cattle kin shrugged and said, "I'm mighty disappointed in an old pal's kid, but Rube says Lawyer Lovecraft was in on that murderous kid's escape in Fort Smith. If so, he had it coming. I never retained him to murder anybody and he should have known that when you lie down with dogs you wind up with fleas."

He drained his schooner. As Mister Horn handed him another Big Dutch declared, "I wish you well but, like I said, it ain't my fight."

It might not have been diplomatic to tell a cattle king backed by that many hands to go fuck himself, so Longarm thanked him for his time, thanked Mister Horn for the beer, and got out of there before he could get himself in trouble.

He saw what Rube Shire meant about having to bite your tongue and like it or lump it when you were given no choice. He agreed it galled more, knowing how sure big shots were that you weren't fixing to lump it. It cramped a man inside to think, "One of theses days!" when he knew they knew such a day might never come.

He was still brooding about it as he rode on in the morning, opting to shunpike and cut off that dog-leg along the Wichita by cutting such fences as he needed to and repairing them before he rode on. Splicing bob wire took less time than a mile out of one's way.

Poor Buscadero was fixing to founder and Longarm sent for Doc Wieder the vet as they rubbed the lathered barb down at the stable behind his hotel.

The shabby-dressing but successful enough old-timer showed up bag in hand to look the chestnut barb over and ask, "Why did you go to so much trouble if you aimed to kill this mount, Deputy Long? Why didn't you just put a gun to his head and blow out his brains?"

Longarm said, "I was in too much of a hurry. Can you do anything for him, Doc?"

The vet shrugged and said, "You and these boys just did about all that can be done, for now. Keep wiping him dry as he cools down, give him water but no fodder for a spell, and wait for equine pneumonia to make up its mind. If it sets in your mount will die. If it don't he'll be needing moderate exercise, bare of back on a paddock lead thrice a day to keep his strained muscles from stiffening. He won't want nobody riding him for at least three days and mind you don't ride him half as hard when you do!"

Longarm said he was much obliged and asked the vet what he owed for the visit. Doc Wieder said a dollar would do him and as Longarm paid the old-timer casually added, "You missed all the exitement, earlier. Rube Shire is a pal of yours, ain't he?"

Longarm said, "He is. I was fixing to scout him up as soon as I took care of my mount and hired another room, here. You know where he might be, right now, Doc?"

Doc Wieder nodded and said, "Over to Doc Ballard's drugstore. Or down below it, least ways. They're holding an inquest on that Tinker Kid as soon as Ballard finished the autopsy."

"The Tinker Kid is dead?" blinked Longarm. He asked, "When did this happen, and what happened?"

Doc Wieder said, "Your pal, Rube Shire, shot him. Happened just this afternoon, over by the Sam Houston Saloon. Rube says he'd been hunting high and low for the rascal when they met up in a blinding flash of mutual recognition and a quick draw contest."

The local vet smiled at the picture as he added, "Don't never side-draw a single action against a man packing double action in shoulder holsters. It just won't work."

Longarm whistled and allowed he'd best go see for himself.

As the two of them left the stable Doc Wieder said, "Ain't that much to see, the way I heard it. Tinker Kid had barely drawed and never got off one round from his old thumb buster before old Rube put three rounds in him, all three fatal, according to Doc Ballard."

Chapter 16

Longarm got there too late for the inquest. Doc Ballard's ad hoc coroner's jury had gone along with his autopsy report and the deposition of the winner and most of them had reassembled in the Sam Houston to make certain they'd pictured the already legendary gunfight accurately.

Longarm found Rub Shire bellied to the bar with Doc Ballard, Sheriff Maguire and other county dignitaries. Rube Shire waved him over and asked if he'd heard.

Longarm said, "Doc Wieder told me. What happened?"

Rube looked pained and replied, "Lord have mercy I've been over it to where my jaw hurts! Let him read my deposition, Doc."

Ballard handed Longarm a carbon copy typed on onion skin paper as he and Shire made room for Longarm between them at the bar. Shire asked what he was having.

Longarm said, "Let me read this where the bar top's dry, first. I asked most of the way back from Singer's Wells and nobody had seen a tall frosty lady riding with two young squirts of any description."

Rube said, "I asked ahead of you. Nobody spotted 'em on the trail and nobody had seen them here in town until this very afternoon, when all of a sudden I stood face to face with the Tinker Kid out front!"

"How did you know one another?" asked Longarm.

Sheriff Magire said, "We've been studying on that. Has to be someone in town in cahoots and hiding them out. They'd have been noticed at any of our few public flops and somebody must have pointed Rube, here, out to the Tinker Kid."

Shire said, "Could have been Miss Fraw Lion spotted me from hiding. She knew me from The Springs and knew I'd be after her after I'd busted in as she was murdering Longarm, here."

He made a wry face and added, "I'm still counting the ways The Tinker Kid could have won and they're all as depressing. I had no idea who *he* was when there he stood, snarling like a cornered rat and slapping leather!"

He waved his beer schooner at the front glass and went on, "Had he been smart enough to just step around and back-shoot me I'd have had no chance. It was close enough as it was. He tried to draw first and damned near did!"

Sheriff Maguire told Longarm, "Warned you Rube was a damnyankee carpetbagging State Police cuss. Didn't you tell me that Tinker Kid was said to be a quick draw artist, Longarm?"

Longarm went on scanning the deposition as he absently replied, "You hardly ever hear any outlaw with any rep described as *slow*. You say he upped to you in the street out front, Rube?"

Shire said, "Out of nowhere. I wasn't paying any mind to gunfights as I crossed the street out front. There was this wagon loading or unloading out front and as I circled 'round it there he was, coming the other way. Things happened after that like one of them dreams. You know the kind where you're trying to move your arms and legs and it feels as if you're a bug stuck in a jar of honey?"

There came a murmur of agreement. There couldn't have been a man there who hadn't had that nightmare. Rube Shire said, "I must have been moving faster than I thought."

Another man there said, "He sure as shit was! Everything happened in a drumroll of gunshot and as I jumped out of my skin and spun around there stood Rube in swirling smoke and there lay the loser at his feet. Must have been eight or ten shots."

Before Longarm could ask, Shire said, "Six. I got off three from each gun. I know I only put three rounds in him. What can I tell you? I was . . . excited."

Sheriff Maguire said, "I know the feeling. Don't you, Longarm?"

A man who'd killed his first teenaged opponent at a pretty place called Shiloh only nodded. Old war stories could sound like old bore stories to those who hadn't been there and those who'd been there knew how many shots are fired for every one that hits anything.

He knew Rube's deposition would agree near enough with those of other witnesses. He'd read enough to know no two witnesses ever saw things the same way. There was a law school experiment where a kid from another class ran into the room, hurled a bucket of confetti at the professor and ran out laughing.

Then the startled students were asked to describe in writing what they'd just witnessed. A class of say thirty generally wrote down thirty different descriptions of the intruder and what he'd done in front of them all.

Handing the deposition back, Longarm said, "I'll have a plain draft. Ain't ready to fall down yet. I only feel like doing so."

Rube Shire said, "We were talking about another dragnet. Miss Fraw Lion and Frank Hungerford are still out there, somewheres *close*!"

Another voice in the crowd asked, "What sort of a name is Hungerford? If you ask me it sound like one of them names actors make up for themselves!"

Longarm said, "It likely is. Outlaws make up such names for their fool selves, as if they sprung forth from the sea, like Miss Venus. The Tinker Kid was likely never born Rom and Jackson seems a tad pat for Artistic Algernon. That's another reason I got to get on over to your Western Union. After being stuck out yonder where they've yet to string their wires I feel like one of those monks sworn to silence the one day of the year they let him cut loose!"

But he hung around long enough to finish most of his beer and listen for discordant notes that might not jibe. He didn't hear any. It had been agreed an owlhoot rider nobody had seen in recent memory, anywhere, had materialized on the street out front at four forty-five P.M. to most unwisely slap leather on an experienced gunfighter packing double-action in shoulder holsters. With predictable results.

The question before the house was where the *rest* of them could be.

Longarm considered how they might have made it in from The Wells on his way to the telegraph office.

The modest short-cut he'd risked coming in aboard a jaded mount had proven it would be possible to shunpike in from The Wells across mostly open range. There was no way such an odd trio could have made it all the way along the riverside trail without anybody along the way recalling them.

They'd have had to camp out on the range, away from any trail stops. The picture that came to mind only seemed grotesque until you studied on it. If the three of them rode in with bed rolls and trail supplies planned in advance there was no law of nature saying a middle-aged gal couldn't make camp with two men. The three of them might well have enjoyed it. She had to have had some reason for hiding them out so murderously.

Whether fond of them that way or not, it hardly mattered how odd the three of them might have looked if nobody *saw* them. Since they hadn't been seen in Wichita Falls they were hiding somewhere slick or, just as likely, they'd ridden on.

Owlhoot riders splitting up to leave tangled trails was as old a dodge as there was. In the wake of that disasterous Northfield Raid the James-Younger gang had split up, with the posse catching the Youngers and the James boys getting away. Hungerford, so far, had proven quick to rid himself of awkward baggage, starting with that lawyer known to be his lawyer and that colored pal others were likely to remember.

Parting friendly or abandoning the Tinker Kid to go it alone might have worked slicker had the Tinker Kid acted slicker. Old Rube had said he'd have never thought twice about a total stranger encountered on a busy street. Leaving Hungerford in the company of Fraulein Helga?

Making for the black and yellow Western Union sign ahead, Longarm mused under his breath, "Stern-looking older woman in the company of a cuss who reminds everybody of a spoiled brat? Coming, Mother, got our train tickets right here and we're off for either coast?"

He strode into the telegraph office and helped himself to a pencil on a chain and a bunch of night letter forms. Western Union let you send more words at lower rates when you let them put them on the wire late at night when business was otherwise slow. Nobody he could wire would be up this late in the evening. So he could afford to word his questions carefully. None of them were all that tricky. He'd simply noticed he didn't really know much about his suspects, starting with what sort of a name Hungerford might be. It did sound made-up, as soon as you thought twice about it.

145

By the time he'd sent off the last of his night letters, paying for all but the update to his home office Henry would sign for, it was on its way to bedtime for folk with steady jobs.

But he figured old Charity wouldn't be too sore if he woke her up for some slap and tickle and, after regaining his strength with Sunny Person, a mediocre white gal seemed a change worth waking up.

When he got to Charity's bungalow, as he'd expected, her lamps out front had been trimmed. But when he walked around to the back, knowing she left her kitchen door un-locked, he spied a soft glow in her bedroom window. She was likely reading in bed, the romantic little thing.

He let himself in the back way, walking mischievously on the balls of his feet to surprise her.

He suprised the shit out of her when he barged in on her and another cuss, going at her dog-style.

Charity gasped, "Custis! Oh, dear, I'm so sorry!"

He said he was too and backed out, shutting the door softly as, behind it, Charity wailed, "Wait! I can explain! I didn't know you were coming back!"

He muttered, "That was for damned sure!" as he de-parted the premises faster than he'd moved in, trying to make up his mind whether he ought to feel outraged or amused.

By the time he'd lit a fresh smoke a couple of street lamps up he'd decided fair was fair and things could have been worse.

Charity could have walked in on him in the same posi-tion with Sunny Person. But it sure beat all how a natural man could feel like gunning another man for just doing what came naturally.

Strolling towards his hotel near the center of things Longarm saw Sheriff Maguire coming from there along with a corporal's squad of other townsmen, a couple of bullseye lanterns and four redbone hounds on leashes.

Maguire told him, "We're fixing to canvas some for the Fraw Lion and young Hungerford, Longarm. Care to join us?"

Longarm said, "Not hardly, and if you mean to run for re-election this November you'll come up sudden with a better way. How would you like somebody to bust in on going at it dog-style, or even worse, acting very friendly with yourself?"

Sheriff Maguire blinked and gasped, "Sweet Jesus on the Water! Are you suggesting young Hungerford might be going at it dog style with that old Fraw Lion?"

Longarm said, "I'm suggesting all sorts of folk could be up to all sorts of shit in the privacy of their own homes, and the Constitution of these United States permits them to. This is Texas, not the Russian Empire, Sheriff. The law can't go tearing through a town like Attila and his Huns just because there's a murderer at large!"

Then how in tarnation are we to *catch* the son of a bitch?" asked one of the would-be searchers backing Maguire's play.

Longarm said, "Same way we always do. The way professional lawmen always have. We got the crooks outnumbered and outpositioned. We're all over, in a position to compare notes and head 'em off no matter where they run. I just now got off a window of wires, asking others all across the land to put their heads together with ours. They can run but they can't hide. Not for long with everybody watching for 'em."

Maguire snapped, "Damn it, Longarm, that's what I just said. That Fraw Lion and her young swain have run some place to hide and I want to root 'em out!"

Longarm said, "You're leaping to conclusions. Who says they have to be lovers? They could be mother and son, or acting like they were. Big Dutch says Fraulein Helga never married and never had any kids. That's one of the things I'm checking. Austin can tell us if she was ever married in Texas. Big Dutch said she came to Texas from their old country."

A spoilsport in the bunch—there always seemed to be one—asked what if an immigrant gal married up and had kids in some other state before she got to Texas.

Longarm said, "Austin won't have a record of it. You eat any apple one bite at a time. You don't expect answers to every question. That's why you keep asking questions."

He turned to Sheriff Maguire and said, "I got one for you, Sheriff. Do you know the name of that secretary gal who worked for Lawyer Lovecraft?"

Maquire said, "That would be Miss Pheobe Byrd. They call her Tweety Byrd. She don't like that, much. She ain't working for Lawyer Lovecraft any more. The poor cuss is dead, remember?"

Longarm said, "I do. That's one of the things I want to talk to her about."

Maguire said, "Tweety Byrd don't know who killed Lawyer Lovecraft. I already talked to her. He sent her home early the day of his murder. She only heard he was dead days later. Same as us. When she came to work the next morning the office was locked tight. She sounded right confused about it when I questioned her. But, then, Tweety Byrd has always sounded right confused, now that I study on it."

Longarm got out his notebook and asked for the secretary gal's home address. Maquire gave it to him, allowing she lived close to the dead lawyer's office.

As Longarm wrote it down, Maguire asked, "You don't mean to pay no call on her at this hour, do you?"

Longarm said, "Not hardly. Don't want to chance catching her in a state of confusion."

Chapter 17

So Longarm got to sleep alone that night. He'd been getting a lot of that lately. Next morning, after checking on old Buscadero, he treated himself to a tub bath and a set down shave and a haircut at the nearby barbershop to kill more than one Byrd with two bits. A small town barber shop had more news for sale than your average small town newspaper and as he waited his turn it was easy to bring up the subject of the late Lawyer Lovecraft and his unemployed secretary.

One of the waiting customers was more up on things. He said he'd heard Tweety Byrd was helping out over at the Grangers' new campaign headquarters. With election coming up after the fall roundup the Granger Party was set to make another try, even though most everybody in Texas had voted Democrat since the end of Reconstruction and the demise of those Black Republican carpetbaggers.

Another speculated on who might replace Lawyer Lovecraft, explaining, "Nobody could beat old W.R. and Miss Tweety Byrd for fast service when it came to the picky pickies of everyday beeswax. W.R. had a lot to learn about complexicated cases. You'd want Lawyer Barnum or mayhaps that Jew, Rothstein, if you were going to *trial*, but young Lovecraft was a caution at cranking out bills of sale, contracts, property deeds or last wills and testaments. Had these thunk-out forms all printed up and Tweety Byrd could fill in the blanks and send you on your way whilst you waited. Most every businessman in town used W.R. and Tweety Byrd for shit like *that*."

That was about all the gossip he picked up that he could use before he left the barber shop feeling tidy, albeit still ready for action on a West Texas scorcher in well broken-in denim.

He asked for directions and they told him the Grangers were set up down the way past the Shire coal yard. So he ankled on down. But before he got there he was hailed by Rube Shire, from the coal yard named after him.

Longarm strolled in to join Rube, a fat Mex and two Anglos, watching a crew of other Mexicans paint rolling stock. They were working on half a dozen assorted milk carts and coal wagons lined up betwixt the main street and the coal piles and tipple to the east. When Longarm asked how come, Shire said, "Aim to neaten things up before I sell it off. I told you I was trying to shed my enterprises this far east of The Wells."

Longarm grimaced and said, "I just spent days on the trail from out yonder. Your point is well taken."

Shire indicated the fat Mex and said, "Gordo, here, is my segundo at both ends of the trail. Been with me since we got started in El Paso. He was the one who got the house greasers out to the Lazy S to tell us about Miss Fraw Lion's other house guests."

The fat Mex didn't seem offended by the Texican endearment, or mayhaps he didn't think greaser applied to him. As he shook with Longarm Gordo said, "Only the *pobrecitas* who worked in *La Casa* for that *bruja* knew about them. Big Dutch has big spread. Most of *La Raza* working for him do not live within sight of his home spread."

The others there were introduced as coal yard workers.

Rube said they'd be working for him out by The Wells once he sold out there in The Falls. Longarm told Rube about his meeting on the trail with Big Dutch and added, "He's either one hell of an actor or didn't know she was hiding those owlhoot riders under his own roof whilst he was over in Fort Worth."

Rube shrugged and allowed, "It could happen. Say he didn't know them on sight if they passed him on the trail as he was coming in. Then say Miss Fraw Lion only meant to hide them like mice whilst the cat was away and send them on to . . . where?"

Gordo said, "New Mexico, perhaps. Is more *ladrones* than one can count over around Las Vegas, even as we speak. There are so many they are now selling stolen stock at ten dollars a head in New Mexico."

It was Rube who pointed out that hardly seemed likely. He said, "If Hungerford and that Tinker Kid had had connections over New Mexico way the three of them wouldn't have headed this way, where Longarm, here, and Sheriff Maguire's whole crew have wants and warrants on 'em."

Longarm frowned thoughtfully and said, "You just now eliminated new thoughts into my head, Rube. It *would* have made more sense for the three of them to blue streak west out of Texas jurisdiction to country I'd have to start all over in. They must have known they were hot as two dollar pistols here in The Falls. So how come you just shot the Tinker Kid here in The Falls?"

"He drew first! Right up the street in front of the Sam Houson!" the former lawman said defensively.

Longarm soothed, "I mean what was he doing in town to begin with. The results of his meeting up with you in broad-ass daylight could have been predicted and should have been predicted. He'd still be alive this very morning if he was over in Las Vegas where nobody knows him."

Gordo proved there was more under his sombrero than one might think at first glance when he asked, "How do we know he was not known in Las Vegas? I just said they were infested with *ladrones* over there. What kind of a name is Rom? I have never met anybody named Rom. Romero, si, is lots of Romeros among my people. Pero the Tinker Kid did not look as if he had much . . . Spanish blood to me."

"Well, he was sort of swarthsome," Rube Shire mused.

Longarm said, "Gypsy. This Gypsy gal I used to know said her kind called one another *Rom* amongst themselves. I might put that questuon on the singing wires when I get the chance. A Gypsy kid who ran away with our kind might have left a trail of memories as he ran. Ain't it a bitch how folk keep changing their fool names as if to confound us all?"

He nodded at a dray being changed from park bench green to funeral black and said, "Might be worth a dollar more, now. I got to get on to Granger Party Headquarters."

It didn't take him long. But when he got there he found no Tweety Byrd there. He introduced himself and explained his needs to the way better looking ash blonde seated at a hauled in desk to register voters. She said, "Miss Byrd didn't . . . quite work out, I fear. To begin with she'd been raised by Black Republicans and didn't seem a very flexible thinker. After that, to be frank, she got on our nerves. Her nickname seemed well-earned."

Longarm said he had Tweety Byrd's home address if push came to shove and, glancing down at her open ledger, observed, "No offense, but you don't seem too busy, here, this morning."

The blonde shrugged and said, "We just got here and November is a long way off. Things will pick up as we recruit a slate of local candidates. Hardly anybody registers to vote for nobody in particular."

Longarm chuckled at the notion but couldn't help observing, "This ain't none of my beeswax, Miss . . . ?"

"Burton, Kitty Burton," she replied.

He went on, "I reckon you know what you're up to, Miss

Kitty. But ain't most Grangers farm folk and ain't this cattle country?"

She said, "The times are ever changing and the Democrat machine you cowboys keep re-electing has nothing new to offer. We Grangers stand for price controls on produce and a square deal for the farm folk who feed the world and . . ."

"Ain't registered to vote in Texas," he cut in, thanking her for her time and getting out of there before she could convert him to the Granger Movement or he could ask to walk her home after work.

When he got to Miss Tweety Byrd's it developed she lived with a tweety old mother, who tweeted her Pheobe was out looking for work in a town that didn't seem to understand the child's sensitive nature.

So Longarm let Tweety Byrd fly off, for the time being, as he found himself understanding her all too well, in mingled annoyance and pity.

Just below the ranks of what poor Charity described as mediocre marched the more pathetic misfits who were *trying* for mediocrity. The ones the other kids had laughed at and always picked last for a game of softball. The ones too educated to dig ditches or clean houses but not sharp enough to hold down a real job and too socially awkward to fit in with the other also-rans.

Lighting a cheroot on the corner, he told the match as he made sure it was out, "Lawyer Lovecraft was laying her or he wanted somebody dumb shuffling his routine papers. So even if I can get her to tell me all she knows about his shady dealing, how much could she know?"

He headed on over to the locked up vacant premises of the murdered mouthpiece. Sheriff Maguire had pasted a notice on the door describing the interior as a murder investigation in progress and forbidding anybody to trespass on pain of prosecution.

So, seeing nobody was supposed to be inside, Longarm

produced a pen knife with a blade refashioned by a Denver locksmith and proceeded to pick the fool lock. It took a spell. The sneaky son of a bitch had bought them a better than average lock.

But all locks were made to be picked if one knew what he was doing and Longarm was soon seated at the late lawyer's desk, going through papers from a drawer he'd had to pick his way into in turn.

He was still going over papers he'd found locked safely away when Sheriff Maguire came in, a big horse pistol in his hand, to say, "Oh, it's you. Old biddy across the way took you for a burglar. Don't let our J.P. hear you busted in with no warrant. Find anything?"

Longarm said, "More elimination. Big Dutch Steinmuller was only listed as a client who payed handsome as hell for no more than consultation. I was told at the barber shop they did a heap of routine business, here but Steinmuller is the only local man of destiny who seems to have retained the youngest lawyer in town."

Longarm started putting papers back where he'd found them as the local law sympathized with him for having wasted his time.

Longarm said, "Time wasn't wasted. That's how you process all your eliminating. Knowing Steinmuller was the only really big account they were handling means Lovecraft wasn't doing much heavy lifting for anybody *else* in these parts."

The sheriff brightened and decided, "Then that ungrateful gun W.R. helped escape the hangman in Fort Smith was the only one with a good motive for killing him. Or any kind of motive, least ways. A man who'd gun pals who trusted him just to silence them would eat shit if you ask me. Had W.R. done any legal chores for that Miss Fraw Lion out to the Lazy S?"

Longarm shut and locked the confidential file as he shook his head and said, "Steinmuller was the only one out at Singer's Wells who ever had Lovecraft do shit for them. Not so mysterious when you consider how far from your county courthouse Singer's Wells is. Steinmuller retained him because he had no lawyer closer, I reckon."

"I think they got more than one courthouse and surely more than one lawyer betwixt here and Singer's Wells," the local law objected, adding, "Lovecraft must have provided . . . more confidential services."

Longarm rose from the desk, saying, "Like everyone in the panhandle and a heap of folk from here, the two of them located from other parts recent. Might be interesting to learn whether W.R. Lovecraft ever practiced law down along the Brazos!"

Sheriff Maguire allowed he'd drink to that as the two of them left together. As Longarm was locking up Maguire mentioned another saloon way closer than the Sam Houston. But they never visited it that morning. For as they stood on the steps out front of Lovecraft's they heard the pounding of hooves and turned to see Big Dutch Steinmuller galloping in with Mister Horn and those other retainers.

Steinmuller spotted them at the same time and set his palomino back on its haunches as they slid to a dusty stop.

The cattle king called, "I want a word with both you birds! Up to the Sam Houston, on the double, whilst we tend to out jaded ponies!"

So the two lawmen headed on up to the Sam Houston. When they got there they found Rube Shire at the bar. Rube said Big Dutch had hailed him in passing and as much as ordered him on to the saloon before noon.

Longarm speculated, "Your shoot-out with the Tinker Kid must have caught up with him on the trail. So he came back."

The former lawman said, "I *had* to gun the fool kid. He slapped leather on me in front of witnesses!"

Maguire said, "Damned A and we're in your corner if they meant to start anything, Rube!"

There came a murmur of agreement from other locals drinking early on a working day. Talk about pending trouble was good for the saloon trade, even if it did slow everything else down in a town that size.

They didn't have long to wait, Big Dutch grumped in at the head of his riders and marched over to that same table, calling out to the barkeep for scuttles of beer and adding, "Longarm, Maguire and Rube in particular. It's time we had some damned cards on the table!"

So they trailed after as the cattle king enthroned himself at the table with his back to the corner and Mister Horn on his feet with a Schofield .45 and an expression of professional servitude.

As Longarm, Maguire and Shire sat down with him, Big Dutch said, "I never met no Tinker Kid. If he was dumb enough to slap leather on a man with a rep wearing shoulder holsters he deserved what he got. So the motion before the house is Helga Reisenfeld and young Hungerford. They were last seen in the company of that trigger-happy Tinker Kid. They should have been long gone by now. But since it seems they may still be nearby I mean to make it plain as day that I am likely to take it mighty personal if anybody Mister Horn and me can get our sights on harms one hair on either of their heads!"

Longarm quietly said, "You said you sent Lawyer Lovecraft to Fort Smith as no more than a favor to an old friend, Mister Steinmuller. Is it safe to say you might have left things out about Fraulein Helga as well?"

The cattle king met Longarm's gaze with his own sharp eyes of twilight blue as he replied in a level voice, "That's for me to know and you not to worry about. Fair is fair and the law is the law. So I won't kill you if Helga and the boy get a chance at a fair trial. But, like I said, I'll take it mighty personal if you bring them in dead, or even badly bruised."

Chapter 18

Longarm sent some wires, going for five cent a word day rates, and canvassed routing up Main Street without cutting any sign worth following up on until all of a sudden the morning was shot and he turned back, figuring on having a look at old Buscadero before he had dinner at the hotel dining room. But when he saw Kitty Burton from the Granger Party on the corner ahead, looking bemused, he joined her with a tick of his hat brim, observing she looked lost, no offense.

The ash blonde, with her hair pinned up under a straw boater at the moment, dimpled up at him to say, "Not lost. Just exploring. This is all so new to me out here. Back home in Maryland it gets hot indoors and out on a day like today. I can't get over how you can go from the oven under the sun to so cool in the shade!"

He said, "Air's dryer and thinner, Miss Kitty. Don't hold the heat so well. I got old friends in Maryland."

She replied, "Really? Where?"

So he smiled sheepishly and said, "Not really. That was an unthinking blurt. We all blurt things that might not jibe with the rest of the tales we tell when we ain't thinking about telling tales."

She laughed and said, So I'm not twenty-nine. Do you know a good place to grab a snack up this way, Deputy Long? I'm on my noon break and feeling peckish."

Longarm gazed about to get his bearings and, spying a familiar awning he said, "My friends call me Custis and that ice cream parlor across the way serves everything from iced black coffee to fattening."

She said, "Oh, let's! I didn't know you could get ice cream this far west."

As he steered her on over he said, "They got them new fangled electrical lights at the Cheyenne Social Club and I know the gent who sells ice to everbody here in Wichita Falls. Things are spread out but not that ignorant in these parts."

He seated her at that same marble top under the awning and Miss Cup Cakes came out to take their orders. Kitty Burton ordered real ice cream, chocolate and vanilla. Being that curvacious at . . . twenty-nine didn't seem to bother her. Longarm allowed he'd have vanilla. Chocolate had been leaving a bad aftertaste, lately.

As Cup Cakes ducked inside, Kitty asked him, "Custis, do you have any idea why that waitress was smirking at us so?"

He said, "She's got some growing up to do. When you're that young you don't just know it all. You know more than there might be to know. Mark Twain makes an interesting observation about that. He writes that when he was twenty he couldn't get over how ignorant his dear old dad was."

She laughed and said, "I read it. Once he was forty he couldn't believe how much the old man had picked up in the past twenty years. Tell me about Maryland, Custis."

He said, "Like I said, it was an unthinking blurt, inspired by a brand of snakebite medicine Maryland is famous for."

She laughed and softly sang

Rye whisky, rye whisky,
I know you of old.
You've robbed my poor pockets,

158

Of silver and gold!

He allowed she had to be from Maryland, seeing she knew their state song. Miss Cup Cakes came out with their ice cream, smirking like Miss Mona Lisa. There was no way Longarm could ask her if Charity and that galoot he'd caught her with had been by, earlier. Longarm felt no call to keep an eye on the bank across the way. He had a clear conscience as far as Charity and, what the hell, Sunny Person, had anything to say about his eating ice cream with anyone in creation. He'd never told *them* they couldn't . . . eat ice cream to their heart's content.

As he ate some with Kitty Burton they got to know one another better, if not in the Biblical sense a man might hope for in such curvaceous company. You couldn't invite a gal to an evening bellied up to the bar and that cake sale shindig lay off in the future. He was about to say he'd heard a German band held evening concerts over by the falls when all hell seemed to be busting loose closer to the center of town.

Kitty said, "What was that? It sounded like gunshots! A lot of gunshots!"

Longarm snapped another silver dollar on the marble and said, "Stay here. You heard correct and I'm the law!"

Without waiting for Kitty's answer Longarm lit off down the street, drawing his own gun along the way as he saw a crowd ahead, gathered over something flatter in the fine dust and powdered horse shit of the sun baked street.

Longarm knew what it was before he got there. An expensive top-of-the-line and snow-white ten-gallon Stetson had been kicked farther out in the dust.

As Longarm elbowed through, gun in hand, to see Big Dutch Steinmuller smiling up at the sky with his eyes closed, as if enjoying a sun bath in a mighty odd place with his boots on. Somebody called out, "Over in the coal yard! Rube Shire and Mister Horn have the son of a bitch cornered!"

So Longarm ran that way with half the town following until he saw Rube and Steinmuller's segundo on his side of that row of carts and wagons with their own guns drawn. Rube Shire called out, "Don't come no closer! I sent Gordo for my rifle and a Greener ten guage!"

Longarm ran on in anyway to hunker down between Rube and the grim-face Mister Horn, tersely asking, "What happened and where is it?"

Mister Horn said, "Big Dutch and me were crossing the street when it happened. He never knew what hit him. He was going down before I knew the single shot I'd heard meant shit!"

Rube said, "I didn't see that much. But when I saw Mister Horn, here, tearing down the street I fell in with him. My segundo, Gordo, waved us this way, pointing over behind that coal. From the way Pablo pictured the kid running past him across this yard, it sounds like it could be that Hungerford you're after!"

Mister Horn growled murderously, "If it was, the ungrateful young bastard paid the man who saved him from a hangman with a shot in the back!"

Rube Shire said, "Don't let on we know. Let me see if we can take him alive."

Rube rose to his feet, staying under cover behind the high sides of a fresh-painted dray, to call out, "Hungerford? We know where you are and you can see there's a twelve-foot board fence with bob wire topping on the far side of you. There's no way you're about to get out from ahint them coal piles or down from that tipple without your weapons preceding you! So why don't you toss out that antique and I promise no one will hurt you without a fair trial!"

"Antique?" asked Longarm.

Rube said, "Gordo said he was waving an old Navy Colt as he tore past. Don't ask *me* how come."

Mister Horn said, "*Sounded* like a .36, now that I study on it. I never got a good look at the sneaky bastard. Had not

160

that Mex spotted him he might have gotten clean away with his daddy's war relic!"

Rube yelled some more as a heap of Wichita Falls listened from a safe distance. After trying a few more times, Rube said, "He ain't coming out. I'm going in."

Longarm said, "Hold on. There's hours of hungry and thirsty daylight left to work with and have you noticed we're dealing with a killer of the cold-blooded persuasion, Rube?"

Rube Shire said, "He's rattled. He's alone. I say strike whilst the iron is hot, before his pals can come to help him out!"

"What pals, that crazy Fraulein Helga?" asked Longarm as Shire broke cover to move in along the fence line to the north. Mister Horn said, "Cover me!" as he crabbed south to that fence line. So Longarm muttered, "Aw, shit!" and busted out from between two coal wagons to charge on across the gritty yard and flop at an angle on the far slope of gritty coal.

He felt pretty sure Hungerford wasn't up in that coal tipple they used to load delivery wagons sudden. For had he been, he'd have fired at one or the other of them by this time.

"See anything?" called Rube Shire from down his way.

Longarm called back, "If he ain't up in the tipple he must be on the far side of this very pile!"

Mister Horn to his south called, "I see him! See his boot, least ways! You're right, Deputy Long. He's in position to blow your face off it you crawl on over! Stay put and let me see what I can do from here!"

Mister Horn fired from the south. At the same time Rube Shire made a mad dash along the north fence line, suddenly dropped to one knee and held his Colt Lightning in both hands as he emptied the wheel into something or somebody Longarm couldn't make out.

Mister Horn called, "I think you got him! He ain't moving at all. His boot heel ain't, I mean!"

161

Longarm took a deep breath and followed his gun muzzle over the top. So the three of them could regard what was left of Famous Frank Hungerford. He lay on his side in a fetal position with his Navy Colt cap and ball .36 in hand, the blood oozing from his open mouth, the only thing about him that that wasn't filthy. He looked as if he's been hiding under a house before rolling on coal dust—and that worked when you studied on it.

Rube Shire moved in as if in charge, which he might have been, since it was his coal yard and his shooting that had dropped the rascal.

Rube dropped to one knee, his own gun in hand, and felt the side of Hungerford's neck to announce, "Dead as the snows of yesteryear. Where's Sheriff Maguire?"

The older lawman came around the pile, his own gun drawn, to declare, "Don't ever do that again, Rube. It's a good way to get killed. I sent a boy for the meat wagon. Where'd you nail him?"

Rube said, "Hard to say after the first couple of shots. I hope they come along with that smokeless powder they keep promising. Got my first round off as he was rearing up like a sea lion with that funny old gun!"

Maguire said, "Navy Colt ain't funny when it's firing at you. Old Sam Colt designed it with slaughter in mind. Cap and ball killed a lot of Comanche and Mexicans before it killed even more in the War Betwixt the States and didn't Doc Ballard say both Lawyer Lovecraft and that darky were back-shot .36 caliber?"

As he examined both bodies later in the day, Doc Ballard found a mushroomed front-loaded .36 slug in the cadaver of Big Dutch Steinmuller. Somebody had crisscrossed the soft lead tip with knife cuts to make it expand in the wound. Doc Ballard held that such a spine shot would have done Steinmuller in without the artistic overtones. Mister Horn had guessed right. Steinmuller never

162

could have known what hit him, unless a hanged man feels something after that sudden snap.

As in the case of the Tinker Kid, for all his firing, Rube Shire had only put two bullets in Hungerford's chest. But either one would have been enough. Longarm had no call to observe a lot of men kept on firing after they couldn't see the target. It wasn't such a dumb notion. You could be in a whole lot of trouble if the cuss you'd thrown down on was still alive in all that smoke.

Doc Ballard called the hearing for after supper time, after he'd settled his nerves and studied on what he'd been up to down in his cellar. Part-time coroners weren't as used to the grim chores as big city full-timers.

When they'd heard the doc's autopsy findings, on top of the not mismatching testimony of everyone who'd been anywheres near the noisy affair, the panel held Steinmuller's death to be premeditated murder most foul and Hungerford's to be more than justified. Had Rube Shire been less modest, they'd have held a torchlight parade in his honor that evening. But he settled for some celebrating at the Sam Houston. Gordo was invited, even if he was a fat greaser. For had Gordo not spotted Hungerford in full flight, the murdersome little shit might have gotten clean away. Nobody had the least notion where that Fraw Lion could be. So wherever they'd been holed up had to be something else.

More than one man there, in spite of Longarm's reservations about Constitutional Law, was for just holding a township-wide short-arm inspection, with everybody required to come out and expose every secret they had, including genital sores, 'til they had some law and order round The Falls.

Wiser heads prevailed when Doc Ballard suggested the late Famous Frank might have been hiding in a prairie dog hole with that dirty old gal. He said that under more recent coal dust and blood stains the body had had ground-in dirt under its fingernails and in its hair, like you'd pick up living in a poorly made sod house or one of those caves kids were forever devising in vacant lots.

He elaborated, "You know that kind where the neighborhood kids dig a pit in the 'dobe, lay a land office sign or a stolen barn door over it, and then cover the same with dirt? Must be more than one such kid stunt in a six-by-six mile township, with some forgot by kids outgrowing them, covered over with this summer's bunch grass or weeds."

Sheriff Maguire decided dragnetting vacant lots would cost him way fewer votes that fall than going house to house and they were still at it when Longarm left, feeling like he'd been rolling in vacant lots or yards for Pete's sake.

He went back to his hotel, stripped down, and treated himself to a whore's bath at the corner stand. He'd just finished when there came a sort of timid knock at the door.

Hoping it was somebody on his side, Longarm wrapped a towel around his hips and followed his sixgun over to see who it might be.

It was Kitty Burton. The political party gal didn't seem to notice his state of *deshabille* as she said, "I hope you won't think me bold, Custis. But I'll never get to sleep tonight in such a strange town if nobody tells me what on Earth has been going on!"

So Longarm said, "Come on in, then. I wouldn't want you to stay awake all night, Miss Kitty."

Chapter 19

By the time he'd satisfied her curiosity with a full relation of all he knew, administered with sips of Maryland snakebite medicine, Kitty had commenced to satisfy a heap of Longarm's curiosity about her and one of the first curious things he found out about her was that she was not ash blond all over. But he had to admire a gal who put that much time and trouble and peroxide into self-improvement.

As they were cuddled to get their wind back with the aid of snakebite medicine and a shared cheroot, Kitty asked if he thought Rube Shire could be talked into joining her Granger Movement.

He said, "I can ask him for you. But I understand he'd been shedding Wichita Falls in favor of another settlement out on the panhandle. If I follow your drift you and the folk you work for have been wondering how vulnerable the local machine's sheriff may be, come November, right?"

She shrugged a shapely shoulder and replied, "It's not as if Sheriff Maguire has done anything but run in circles since that local lawyer's murder and we've been given to understand Rube used to be a member of the Texas State Police."

Longarm cuddled her closer and put the hotel tumbler

of branch water and snake medicine to her lips as he said, "That ain't considered a political asset out this way. I doubt many Texas Democrats would vote for him even if he helped me capture Fraulein Helga."

Kitty murmured, "Ooh, that's right! She's still at large, if not the mastermind behind all this mad dog killing! So even though the three fugitives you were after have all been killed, you can't return to Denver until you tie up the loose ends and I'm so glad!"

He kissed the part of her hair and murmured, "I ain't in that much of a hurry to leave, since taking this sudden interest in the Granger Movement. But I'd sure like to know how that strange old gal fits in. Big Dutch told me there was nothing going on betwixt them."

She pointed out, "He lied about his interest in Frank Hungerford, too. Didn't you just tell me that after dismissing the young wastrel as the son of an old friend he threatened to kill anyone who harmed a hair on the boy's head?"

Longarm said, "On Fraulein Helga's head as well. Mayhaps he felt a tad sheepish, the way a sheep herder might, I mean. She must have been mighty devoted to *him*. I can still taste it. She stood ready to murder a federal lawman in cold blood to save that lad Big Dutch had only a casual interest in."

He took a drag, blew a thoughtful smoke ring, and decided, "Whatever the interest was, Fraulein Helga was devoted to Big Dutch and must have known what it was. Devoted help always does. They say no man is a hero to his valet, what with the valet tending to his dirty underwear and lacing him into his corset if need be. I'm sure she'd be able to tell us more than that autopsy could, if only I could locate her."

She reached down between them as she allowed she hoped it was fixing to take him a spell. As he got rid of the tumbler and cheroot to roll back in her love saddle he had

166

to allow he meant a thorough investigation of the case before he hauled out.

They wound up on the floor with her on top. Snakebite medicine could have that effect on curvacious bottled blondes who'd been lonesome in a strange town.

Kitty confessed as much, back up on the bed, once sanity returned as they nursed some rug burns with a hotel towel dipped in Maryland Rye.

She said, "Until you came into my arms out of nowhere I was feeling so left out and greenhorn. It seems everybody out this way have ridden together, as they put it, sharing memories of the long ago, such as that famous Three O'Clock Duster I've heard so much about."

He cocked a brow to ask, "Who said it was all that long ago? I'm new in town and I was there. You must have just missed it by a day or so."

She answered "Really? I'd pictured it around the time of that fight at The Alamo. I heard about it from the janitor sweeping out that store we just rented for our campaign headquarters. He said all that dust he was sweeping out had blown in under the door. He spoke as if explaining the ice age."

Longarm said, "It caught everybody by surprise. Including the killer of Lawyer Lovecraft unless he somehow managed a private dust storm. I could get things to fit together better if I could put that killing *after* the dust storm. I could put a heap of things together better if only I could get them to *fit*. But no matter which picture I try to put together, I keep winding up with pieces that say the contrary."

And so things went for the next three days and nights, with the nights a heap nicer than the days. For the days stayed hot and dry as answer after answer to his wired check-out came in, with heaps of answers that only inspired other questions when some answers seemed to contradict others.

That outdoor dance and cake sale came and went, with Kitty allowing she enjoyed the dancing but wasn't sure she cottoned to some of the fishy looks she got from local gals who didn't know her and had to wonder where she got that summer frock.

The unexpected break he needed came as a bolt from the blue or a sudden urge for something cool on Kitty's part as Longarm took her up Main Street on her noon break and they wound up at that ice cream parlor Miss Cup Cakes smirked at.

Miss Cup Cakes wasn't there. The fat gal who came out to take their order begged their indulgence if she served a tad slow because she was shorthanded in the back.

When Kitty asked how come the fat gal said that snip of a waitress they'd been served by earlier had run off to Fort Worth with a married man who'd payed a heap for that zebra-striped cake the other night.

As she served them sorbet with a lock of her hair down over her eyes she said they'd been searching in vain for a replacement. Longarm didn't ask why. It was the sort of job few wanted if they could sign on as, say, an opera singer.

He took Kitty back to her political hackery and smoked down another cheroot before he decided he had nothing to lose and went to pay a call on Miss Tweety Byrd.

He found the mousy misfit at home, dusting in a work smock as her mother worked as a serious cleaning woman to put bread on their table.

Somebody had to.

Tweety Byrd didn't want to let him in. She protested, "I'm not properly dressed, and there's nobody in the house but me!"

He assured her, "I ain't come a-courting, Miss Mouse, I mean Phoebe."

She tittered and said, "You're being silly. But tell me what you've come for, Mister Froggy."

Standing on her doorstep, Longarm said, "I know where you might be able to get a job. I expect some favors in return."

She blushed beet red and half whispered, "I couldn't! I'm not that kind of a girl!"

He said, "I suspected as much, no offense. I ain't after your fair white body, ma'am. There's things I need to know about the late Lawyer Lovecraft. You went to work for him when he first come up here from the Brazos. No man is a hero to his valet and nobody's secrets are safe with his secretary, if you follow my drift."

She did. She said to come in and served him poorly brewed coffee and stale store-bought cake. But what the hell, the icing was vanilla.

He said, "Found out by wire that before Big Dutch Steinmuller paid your boss that handsome retainer, or expense money, he put him through law school back east. Have you any notion why?"

Sitting down beside him on the love seat, Tweety Byrd said, "I can guess. Lovecraft wasn't his real name. He'd changed his name to a more American-sounding name for business reasons."

"Then his real name was . . . ?" asked Longarm.

When she said Steinmuller he blinked and said, "Of course! He told me his first wife left him during the war. She took the kids and went home to her mother! Could you hazard a guess as to Hungerford's real name?"

She sighed and said, "I don't have to guess. Poor W.R. referred to him more than once as his black sheep."

"Jesus H. Christ, sorry Miss Phoebe, I never pictured things at all that way! But if Lawyer Lovecraft and Famous Frank were brothers, and Big Dutch was their father, every move Big Dutch, Lawyer Lovecraft and even Fraulein Helga made makes sense! But what sort of the blackest sheep would have call to murder the father and brother who'd just saved him from a public hanging?"

"A mighty ungrateful black sheep indeed?" she suggested, adding, "What if he's just crazy mean?"

Longarm said, "He'd have to be, with change left over. But when you eliminate senseless you peel the onion down to means, motive and opportunity. So I want you to get dressed and ask for the job of waitress at the ice cream parlor across from Stockman's Savings & Loan. Before you cloud up and rain all over me, I know it's a kid's job. So how much did you make in tips working for a small town lawyer whose only big client was his own father?"

She jumped up to say she was fixing to apply in her Sunday-Go hat and dress. He rose to take his leave. The next nine hours passed like a cat shitting through a funnel, with Kitty sore about him not taking her home, even though he swore there was nothing going on betwixt him and the new waitress at the ice cream parlor.

Then it was going on ten and the only action along Main Street was piano music spilling out saloon doors as Longarm circled around behind Rube Shire's ice plant like an alley cat, clinging to the shadows.

The loading dock was deserted, with all the doors padlocked and the ice wagons lined up like dominos, wherever the horses might be.

Longarm found a smaller side door and picked the lock with the bullseye lantern he'd brought along at his feet, unlit.

After he'd let himself in he struck a match and lit the lantern. It was called a bullseye because its bitty flame was concentrated by a powerful lens to throw a narrow beam ahead.

It was easy to eliminate where *not* to look. Not bothering with the cavernous storage spaces or the vat room where ice was frozen into big blocks in tanks cooled by brine pipes, Longarm headed for the engine room where all that chilled brine was sent on its way by steam-driven pumps. The steam operation was shut down for the night, ready to start up when needed. It was still warm in there. Longarm moved down into the colder core of the plant, where expanding ammonia chilled brine down to colder than fresh-water ice. Nothing was moving back there. It was quiet as a tomb and colder than a banker's heart. As he swung the beam about he saw a work bench and some crates frosted white as cake icing by the constant cold back there. He nodded and followed his bullseye beam over to the piled crates. There was nothing in the one atop the pile. He set it aside and opened the crate it had been sitting on. He was braced for it. But it still gave him a turn when he opened the lid to see Fraulein Helga staring back at him, seated as if in a tub with all her riding habit and everything else about her sugared with frost.

He murmured, "Evening, ma'am. You just stay put whilst I rustle up the sheriff and his boys."

As he shut the lid a voice behind him asked, "Lose something, Longarm?"

He turned to see Rube Shire standing there with a double action .38 Lightning in one hand and that .36 Navy Colt in the other, illuminated spooky by the lantern at Longarm's feet.

Longarm said, "Found what was missing, Rube. Would you care to hear how you fucked up your perfect crime?"

Rube replied in a surprisingly conversational tone, "I sure would. Who told you? You never figured it out for yourself. Nobody was smart enough to figure it out for himself!"

Longarm said, "My first clue was all that dust on Hungerford. Makes it certain you got on to that other devious plan to free Hungerford and you saw the chance to be the Texas answer to Allan Pinkerton and whup Sheriff Maguire in the coming election."

Shire said, "Bullshit. I was figuring on running out Singer's Wells way as soon as they incorporated."

Longarm said, "Bullshit right back at you. I checked

171

with Austin. Ain't enough voters out yonder to incorporate a county. You were two-facing Maguire as you worked to show him up and get yourself drafted to run against him, you modest thing."

Shire said, "Whatever," and waved one of his sixguns at the crate Fraulein Helga was sitting in, adding, "Get on with it. Tell me how clever I was, you big federal sleuth."

Longarm said, "You cut yourself in as a two-faced confederate or just a hang-about as Lawyer Lovecraft waited here in The Falls to take delivery on Hungerford. Before they ever arrived in that delivery dray they stole in Fort Smith you back-shot their lawyer with that distinctive murder weapon and ran him out of town in *another* dray of your own. Fort Smith wired the dray stolen there was made by Baker Brothers. Same as that park bench green dray over in your coal yards. Lawyer Lovecraft was left dead in that dray made by the Fisher Company. Later that same night, when the three outlaws arrived in the real stolen dray, you put all three on ice, dusty as they were, to be taken out in turn as you staged you heroics."

"Then who tried to murder you out at the Lazy S?" Rube demanded.

Longarm answered simply, "Faulein Helga, acting alone out of misguided loyalty to a man she loved and his black sheep son. She was afraid I was getting warm. The three oulaws you had on ice never made it out yonder. Nobody from the Lazy S ever told me they had. Like a lot of practiced liars you cited witnesses you knew I'd never check with. When I passed out the inexperienced murderess was panic-stricken and turned to you for help, having heard you were working with Lovecraft-Steinmuller. I would have been little use to you dead so you double-crossed her as well and saved my life, and for that I thank you. You had Gordo run her into town to hide her out and yonder she's still hiding, on ice. I bought your bullshit out at The Wells because it seemed to hold together and well . . . Because I liked you."

Rube said, "I liked you, too. Sorry things had to end this way. But quit your stalling and tell me who told you what was really going on!"

Longarm said, "Nobody had to, soon as I found out something you could not have known when you plotted your devious plot. That ungrateful hired gun you were selling us all just wouldn't work as soon as I found out he was the brother of the lawyer he murdered and the son of the sponsor he paid back with a bullet in the back."

"The three of them were *kin*?" gasped the liar who'd killed all three of them. Then he asked, "Does anybody else know?" and Longarm answered, "Not so far," before he wondered why anyone would want to say a dumb thing like that!

Chapter 20

Longarm kicked the lantern and dropped as it went skittering off across the cold tiles without going out like it was supposed to. The infernal machine had been invented with rough handling in mind, and its beam swept in every direction in imitation of a toy lighthouse gone mad whilst Rube Shire blazed away with both sixguns, confounded by the razzle-dazzle effect on his own billowing clouds of cotton-white black-powder smoke, until of a sudden the beam was stationary, pointing straight up, and Longarm fired once from where he lay on his side on the tiles.

Once was enough when you knew what you were doing.

Rube Shire said, "Aw, hell, I think I'm dead," and never said another word as he pitched forward through the swirling smoke to land on his face with the grace of fresh cow pat.

Longarm fired again as Gordo tore in, yelling, *"Ay que chihuahua, que pasa?"* followed by, *"Ay, mierda, me jodi!"* as it came to him he'd run right into a round of .44-40.

Longarm rose stiffly from the cold tiles, covering Gordo with his smoking sixgun as the fat Mex tried to hold himself erect but slid down the door jamb to end up like a seated Buddha in a spreading pool of steaming blood.

Longarm asked, "Is this a private party or might any number be coming to play? Tell me true and tell me sudden, lest I gut shoot you some more, Gordo!"

The Mexican stared up reproachfully to reply, "If I knew where my gun went I would kill you. *Ese pendeja pistola se me salte de me fregada mano* as if she had a life of her own. Have you seen her, *amigo mio?*"

Longarm said, "We were talking about how many others were backing Rube's play. You couldn't have been the only *carnal* he trusted with his secrets, *solo!*"

The gut-shot Gordo pouted, "For why could I not be *el segundo solo?* You take me for *estupido*? You dare? *Oyes, carnal*, I know how to read and *me patron* said he was *dependiente* on me for to help him. He could never have tricked everybody without me. Am I going to die?"

Longarm calmly said, *"Sin falta*, but first you have to tell me how you worked that public shoot-out with The Tinker Kid, seeing you'd just thawed him out for Rube to shoot it out with in public!"

Gordo asked, "For why should I tell you *mierditos?*"

Longarm said, "Don't you want to die famous? Think of how *La Raza* will brag on you, Gordo! Everybody took you for a dumb fat greaser fetching and carrying like some *peon* when all the time you and Rube were slickering the shit out of everybody!"

Gordo chuckled, winced in pain, and settled some as he replied, "Is true. Was most *ingenioso*. The Tinker Kid, as you say, was on ice in one of those crates you see over there until Rube was ready for to shoot it out with him. We thawed him out. Rube put some bullets in him here. This was all done the night before. So nobody working out back would see. We put him in an ice wagon we hid in the carriage house of a vacant place Rube has for sale. As he went on for to be seen other places I drove the ice wagon along Main Street, slow. Who looks twice at an ice wagon? In front of the Sam Houston, Rube came to meet us, both

176

guns making smoke. When was plenty of smoke I dropped the body under the wagon through a hole we had made and drove on. I wish I could have stayed for to watch the act!"

"Who left the bodies of Lovecraft and that colored rider down along the Wichita?" Longarm asked.

Gordo sighed and said, *"Me duele la barriga*, that *hijo de puta* shot me *muy malo*. Was easier at the coal yard. *Matador grande* Rube saved for last was left behind coal so I could see him running in off *el camon* after he shot Steinmuller. Was dead for weeks when everyone see you got him trapped for everyone to watch!"

"Was Mister Horn in on it?" asked Longarm.

Gordo said, "I spit in his father's milk. He was stupid as the rest of you and they say he was big range detective. Rube and me had all of you fooled. For why did you blow out that lantern? I can no longer see you and I wish for to find my gun and kill you."

Longarm said, "Hold the thought. I'll see if we can get you to a doc, Gordo."

He made sure he'd gathered up Shire's three pistols and Gordo's Dance Brothers sixgun before he followed his bullseye beam out, leaving the three of them, counting Fraulein Helga, in the frigid darkness.

Out on Main Street, Sheriff Maguire and half the town had been hunting high and low for the source of all those muffled gunshots.

To Longarm's mild surprise they found Gordo still alive inside, in tears because he was afraid of dying in the dark without a padre and because he was starting to really hurt as the shock wore off.

If this was rough on Gordo it was a break for the law, because Doc Ballard, with advice from the horse doctoring Doc Wieder, managed to keep Gordo alive on laudanum for the next few days, laudanum being a mixture of alcohol and opium. Longarm and a pretty good reporter sent by *La Prensa de Fort Worth y Dallas* managed to convince Gordo he might die famous as Joaquin Murieta or Tiburcio Vasquez if he cared to tidy up more loose ends, and Texas was spared the expense and ingenuity of hanging all that lard in the end when old Gordo met his maker after literally spilling his infected guts.

Miss Tweety Byrd helped with other loose ends as she served Longarm ice black coffee and lime sorbet in her newfound position at the ice cream parlor. He'd decided he liked their lime sorbet best and Miss Tweety Byrd said she was making more in tips than she'd earned off a boss whose only big client had been his dad. Miss Tweety Byrd was starting to blossom as she found she'd risen to the level of her competence.

Serving customers at an ice cream parlor where she presented less of a threat to the ladies she served whilst the men she served seldom got fresh and left nickels and dimes for a poor drab who'd come down in the world, in their opinion.

As he wrapped things up in The Falls, Longarm left Buscadero for the wistful Kitty Burton to ride around on, whether getting to know her new surroundings better or distribute literature for her cause.

He gave the yellowboy to Sheriff Maquire, who could always use an extra rifle around the office, and rode back to Fort Worth with that reporter from the Spanish lingo newspaper.

It took him fewer railroad transfers to get on back to Denver, being he was able to circle south of the staked plains aboard the Southern Pacific and connect with a northbound Denver & Rio Grand at El Paso.

He arrived too late in the day to disturb his boss by reporting in and relating all his field adventures to a certain young widow with light brown hair as pillow talk helped to clarify the twisted tale of family secrets and political ambitions in his mind.

So next morning, after a damned fine breakfast in bed

178

up on Capitol Hill, Longarm ankled in earlier than usual, after his home office had been open an hour, to find his boss fuming in the oak-paneled back office because he'd already heard his senior deputy was back in town.

The somewhat older and way shorter and fatter Marshal William Vail shot a weary look at the banjo clock on one paneled wall as he growled, "So nice of you to drop by at last. I read the reports you wired in ahead. I find them mighty confusing. You'd best start at the top and work on down."

Longarm helped himself to a seat in the leather-covered and horse-hair-padded chair Billy Vail never invited him to sit in as he got out a three-for-a-nickel cheroot and lit it in self defense without permission.

A man without better-smelling tobacco smoke up his nose was in mortal danger back there as Billy Vail smoked expensive but evil black stogies behind his cluttered desk.

Longarm began, "Back before the war when he and Texas still had some growing up to do, a second generation High Dutch cowhand married up young and had two kids with a sort of spoiled Texas belle. So he could have stayed out of the war and she felt he should have stayed out of the war, but when he had the chance to be a cavalry officer in Hood's Brigade he rode off to war anyway and she was mad as hell."

"Watch where you flick them fucking ashes!" Billy Vail growled, bidding him to pray continue.

Longarm said, "Tobacco ash is good for carpet mites and I keep begging you to set up a fucking ash tray over this way. But I digress. The young Captain Steinmuller's woman went home to mother and by the time he got home from the war things down Texas way made it hard enough for a man with nothing to show for it all but a Confederate Discharge printed on wallpaper to feed himself. The already teenaged boys stayed put for a spell with their mother's rich kin."

He flicked more ash and said, "Steinmuller remarried and got on with getting rich, himself, along the Brazos. Had a natural way with livestock and treated his help right, inspiring devotion and the sort of attention to chores such devotion inspires. Along the way he hired another High Dutch immigrant who reminds me in a way of that Miss Byrdy I'll get to in a minute. Fraulein Helga acted hell on wheels but she was a misfit all her life until she found her calling as the utterly devoted housekeeper of a man who could have had her cherry, only he never did. Doc Ballard was able to establish that when he autopsied her."

"You wired she was crazy, too," nodded Vail.

Longarm said, "Not crazy crazy, just overly devoted and you're getting me ahead of the damned story. So let's go back to where Big Dutch moved his cattle operations up to more wide open spaces on the tidied up panhandle range. By this time both his boys were grown up and as many a divorced parent has learned, more willing than their momma to forgive Big Dutch for her divorcing him. He put the elder son through law school. The younger one had grown up too wild for any sort of higher education. He took up assassination for hire as his career, whilst the lawyer son followed their dad north to be his lawyer in the nearest town of any size."

"Damn it, Custis, I've a mind to make you sweep that carpet!" his boss cut in, adding, "Then the father and the obedient son heard their black sheep was fixing to attend a mass hanging in Fort Smith. Where does Rube Shire fit in?"

Longarm said, "He never, far as Big Dutch was concerned. He backed young Lawyer Lovecraft, as they called him, with plenty of money and sent him to get his kid brother off by hook or by crook. After he'd failed in court before Judge Parker, who must have been amused by his optimism, W.R. recruited a pair of outlaws he'd defended with more luck along the Brazos and sent them to do what we all know they done. They slickered me, gunned those

180

Fort Smith deputies, and lit out in that stolen dray of park-bench green. I never saw it, as I hope you recall. I tried to head 'em off by rail as they shunpiked through the Indian Territory. Meanwhile W.R. thought he was enlisting the help of a drinking buddy who'd bragged some on being a gun for hire down on the border. That turned out to be a big mistake."

Longarm took a deep drag, blew the smoke out both nostrils like a chagrined bull, and said, "It's tough for normally ambitious men like you and me to savvy the drive that makes some men rich and powerful beyond avarice. I recall this evening up in Leadville when I won big at poker and felt obliged to share my luck by springing for a round of nightcaps. This one old mining magnate addressed me with tears in his eyes as he said he liked me and felt sad as hell I'd never be rich. When I asked him how he could be so certain he said I was too easy to please. He explained that had he won such a swell pot he'd have gone home with his guts tied in knots, wondering if he might not have won more, had he played things even better."

Billy Vail nodded his bullet head and said, "Vice President Colfax must have been a sick puppy, risking ruination for bribe money after he made *segundo* to the top of the totem pole. So Rube Shire was ambitious. Then what?"

Longarm said, "When W.R. turned to him for help in getting his black sheep brother out to the panhandle past that Ranger station in one of his many freight wagons, Rube saw the chance to be a heroic lawman and mayhaps recover the position he'd lost to political changes. He was two-facing his other pal, Sheriff Maguire, as well. He and his devoted Gordo murdered W.R. ahead of time and left him out in that barley field in a delivery dray. They knew the three fugitives would come along in another one just like it, or close enough, before I checked with Fort Smith. They never planned on the black sheep son and his pals coming in through that wild dust storm, but it likely made it tougher for anybody else to notice as Rube made them welcome, told Gordo to hide their dusted up transportation and invited them in for some poison. Then he and Gordo put the three of them on ice until they were needed to confuse the shit out of me and make Rube Shire look good enough to get drafted to run for Sheriff later this fall. He used that distinctive Navy Colt or his own .38 Lightings, as called for, to put artistic bullet holes in all five men and one woman he murdered in the end."

Vail asked, "Clear my head about that Fraw Lion."

Longarm said, "Things out to the Lazy S didn't go quite the way Rube told me they had. I was unconscious at the time and had to take his word for things that never took place."

He flicked more ash and explained, "They really saved my life. Poor misguided Fraulein Helga set out to murder me after Rube told her the black sheep was hiding. As she had me dying on the floor, she thought, Rube had Gordo run her into town to wait for Big Dutch there whilst he, Rube, tidied up. They had to talk her into the long ride across open range to keep her from spoiling before they could put her on ice. Rube meant to catch her last as he wrapped up the case neither the sheriff nor me had been able to crack. After he'd suckered the shit out of me and had us all set up for his grand finale he shot the only man, he thought, who could still spill the beans about W.R. being in on the Fort Smith escape."

"But he didn't know three of his victims were kin!" said Vail. Longarm nodded. "He'd have had to write his drama different if he had. Blood being thicker than water."

He flicked more ash and said, "The rest you know, if you've been paying a lick of attention. A lot of loose pieces suddenly fit as soon as I saw how unlikely a killer Hungerford-Steinmuller made."

Vail said, "I reckon, as far as events up to the dying confession of that fat Mex carried us. But you filed all that by wire over a week ago and it couldn't have taken you no full week to get back up here from Texas, dammit. What took you so long?"

Longarm shrugged, flicked more ash, and tried, "You used to ride down Texas way. You tell me why rail lines run so few and far between down yonder."

Vail said, "Don't try to teach your granny to suck eggs, or lecture an old Texas Ranger about Texas railroad connections. Tell me more about this Miss Tweety Byrd you found so helpful. What did she look like, you sly dog?"

Longarm soberly replied, "Like a mouse in a waitress uniform. You have my word as an enlisted man and a gentleman I never fooled with that witness, boss."

And that was the pure truth when you studied on it, and since old Billy had never asked about Señorita Consuela Estrada y Morales of *La Prensa de Fort Worth y Dallas* Longarm felt no call to go into that part of his field mission.

Watch for

LONGARM AND THE RAILROAD MURDERS

the 328th novel in the exciting LONGARM series
from Jove

Coming in March!

GIANT-SIZED ADVENTURE FROM AVENGING ANGEL LONGARM.

LONGARM AND THE DEADLY DEAD MAN
0-515-13547-X

LONGARM AND THE BARTERED BRIDES
0-515-13834-7

Explore the exciting Old West with one of the men who made it wild!

(Ad # B112)